ARCTIC ASSIGNMENT

What was the secret of desolate, Soviet-controlled Barren Island in the Arctic Sea? What happened to the Lapp Eskimo who visited Barren and never returned? What was the eyeless steel monster that terrified his fellows? Counter-espionage sent a top agent to investigate. He vanished. Clearly, no possible cover story would protect the next British agent to arrive, but someone had to find the answers. Counter-espionage chose a killer — they sent Simon Larren.

ROBERT CHARLES

ARCTIC ASSIGNMENT

Complete and Unabridged

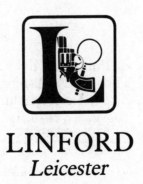

LINFORD
Leicester

First published in Great Britain in 1966

First Linford Edition
published 1998

British Library CIP Data

Charles, Robert, *1938*–
    Arctic assignment.—Large print ed.—
Linford mystery library
    1. Detective and mystery stories
    2. Large type books
    I. Title
    823.9'14 [F]

ISBN 0–7089–5264–X

Published by
F. A. Thorpe (Publishing) Ltd.
Anstey, Leicestershire

Set by Words & Graphics Ltd.
Anstey, Leicestershire
Printed and bound in Great Britain by
T. J. International Ltd., Padstow, Cornwall

This book is printed on acid-free paper

1

An Agent Vanishes

The snow screamed into Cleyton's face like a furious swarm of diving white hornets, attacking with merciless ferocity. His eyes flinched behind his protective goggles and regardless of whether he kept them open or closed he was still blind. There was nothing but the swirling white flakes ripping through the feeble grey swathe cut by the beam of the heavy torch in his thickly-gloved hand, and beyond the howling blackness of the storm-lashed Arctic night.

He had to lean steeply forwards to stop the force of the blizzard from blasting him over on to his back, and he had the grim feeling that if he once fell then the weight of his thick snow-laden furs would never allow him to rise again in the face of the wind. The sound of the blizzard shrieked and stabbed at his eardrums as the wind gusts ricocheted among snow dunes and crags of ice. The unaccustomed snow-shoes dragged clumsily at his feet as he endeavoured to lurch forwards but he was making a minimum of progress. In fact, he doubted whether he was making any progress at all. He knew he had to turn back.

The blizzard had blown up unexpectedly an hour after he had left the small settlement of Stadhaven on Dog Island, a small spot of land in the Arctic Ocean above Norway's North Cape. He was only half-way to his destination, a deeply indented, frozen cove on the west side of the island, and now he bitterly resented the fact that he had to give up the attempt as a wasted effort. The fact that it was very unlikely that there would be anything left to see if he ever did reach the fiord did little to soothe his vexation, and even if there was he failed to see the connection between a shoal of dead fish washed up above the moving ice floes at the mouth of the fiord, a missing Eskimo and the recently-reported Russian activity on the neighbouring Soviet territory of

Barren Island five miles away. But he had to start somewhere, and now he hated to turn back only to face the gruelling trek all over again once the storm had ceased.

He stopped with his shoulders hunched forward and his head bowed to let the storm batter the top of his hooded parka instead of hitting him full in the face, and reverted to what for him was a rare outlet. He swore, very slowly and precisely with a deliberate pause between each sour word. Why, he asked himself disgustedly, did the blasted Russians have to start playing at 'mysterious activities' in this freezing, God-forsaken speck of nowhere? Why couldn't they play their silly bloody games somewhere where it was warm and comfortable? And why did Smith have to pick on him for this particular mission? He began to wish that he had studied Tahitian or Swahili in his youth instead of learning Russian and Norwegian, and turned wearily back.

The moment he stopped leaning into the wind and twisted his ungainly feet around in the snow, the blizzard blew him flat on his face. He swallowed an almost violent swear word and struggled to his hands and knees. The driven snow hurled itself in tearing gusts at his back and threatened to push him down on to his face again as he raised one gloved hand to wipe the freezing slush from the eye-pieces of his goggles. The over-hanging fur hood of his parka was flapping wildly and the wind roared past him as though a continuous express train was thundering by on either side of his crouching figure. He fought his way gamely to his feet in the slipstream of the non-existent trains, and leaned his shoulders into the blizzard to prevent himself being blown forwards again. His feet were braced apart and he moved the grey beam of the torch that he still retained through the savage, swirling nightmare of darkness.

His footprints were already wiped out and the cold tightened around his throat. His numbed fingers moved the torch slowly but without hope. There was nothing to show him the way back to the settlement.

He knew that he should have taken

the advice he had been given before he started out and allowed one of the short, wiry little Eskimo hunters to accompany him. But there had been no sign of a blizzard then, and he had been too uncertain of what he might find to welcome company. Now he knew that he had made a mistake. Dog Island was only small, a mere six miles by ten, but that provided sixty square miles in which to wander round in circles until he froze to death. It was true that he had a very efficient compass strapped to his left wrist, but in this howling muck he could pass within ten yards of Stadhaven and still miss it.

However, there was nothing he could do but start back and hope for the best. He shivered as he checked his direction with the aid of the torch and then headed south-east. He could quite easily have ran all the way with the storm lashing his back to carry him on, but there were so many cracks and fissures across the ice that he dared not move too fast. He slid his snow-shoes forward in clumsy steps, aiming his torch beam just ahead of his feet, and tried not to think of the biting cold that had cut through his furs and was now gnawing at his bones.

For a moment he wondered whether this might have been the way that Tunkut disappeared, but then he remembered that the missing Eskimo had vanished at sea and not on land. And according to reports there had been no foul weather at the time. Tunkut had left Stadhaven in his kayak after announcing his intention of hunting walrus on Barren Island, and had not come back. Now Cleyton was beginning to realise that there were plenty of good reasons why a man should vanish in this inhospitable part of the world without blaming anything on to the Russians at all. It was beginning to look as though he too was going to fail to return.

He wiped more slush out of his goggles and strained his eyes to spot any sudden gaps in the ice ahead, and at the same time allowed his mind to concentrate on Tunkut in an effort to keep the awareness of the ever-increasing cold from taking complete domination.

Taken on its own the disappearance of the lone Eskimo would most probably have been accredited to some natural disaster. He had gone on a walrus hunt and walrus could become notoriously dangerous when wounded or enraged. Some of the bigger bulls weighed several tons and reached a length of twelve feet, and their savage tusks could quite easily smash a small kayak or gore a slow-moving man.

But Tunkut's disappearance was not an incident on its own. The pilot of a small reconnaissance aircraft operated by the fisheries department of the Norwegian Government had reported a newly-constructed landing stage on Barren Island, plus other slight but definite signs of occupation, only a few days before the Eskimo had vanished. And since then other hunters from Dog Island had been terrified by a great monster rearing up from the freezing seas between the two islands, described by the frightened islanders as a huge blind and eyeless whale with a strange, high hump upon its back. The monster could only have been a submarine. But what was a submarine doing in these waters? And what were the Russians doing on Barren Island? And, perhaps least of all, what had happened to the simple Eskimo hunter?

Cleyton had no idea — but he was supposed to find out. And so he had looked with interest upon another unusual event that had stirred the normally routine conversation of the island's inhabitants; the discovery of a whole shoal of dead fish washed up on the west shore — the shoreline that faced the Soviet island across the straits.

The force of the blizzard had heightened now and the wind screamed like a thousand tortured banshees in the black maelstrom of the night, the long below-zero night of the pitiless Arctic. The crippling cold beat all thoughts of his mission from Cleyton's mind and he stumbled forwards blindly, caring less and less about the danger of breaking an ankle or a leg in some concealed fissure in the snow and ice as he realised that if he failed to find Stadhaven soon then he would die. His fingers and toes were already numb and every muscle in his body ached. He cursed again at the startling speed and fury with which the blizzard had arrived.

He could see nothing now, surrounded by the roaring, rushing darkness of gale-blown snow, hearing only the wailing agony of the wind and feeling nothing but the vicious buffeting at his shoulders and the inexorable advance of the cold. He knew that it was time he checked his direction again and braced himself with difficulty as he fumbled to direct his torch at his compass. Fresh gusts of snow swept thickly across his line of vision and he had to bow his head close to the face of the dial before he could read it. He saw with relief that he was still on the right course, and then a combination of swamped sound, vague movement and instinct made him suddenly realise that he was no longer alone.

He swung the torch away from his compass, arcing it through the racing, grey, snow-clouds as fast as his clumsy fingers would allow. He almost dropped it in his haste and then the beam picked out a looming shape in encumbering furs, the short squat shape of an Eskimo.

Cleyton gasped a muffled sob of thanks into the thick coverings that protected the lower half of his face from frost-bite and made to move forward. He was offering a silent prayer to the counter-espionage equipment officer who had provided him with the accurate compass to bring him on a straight line back to Stadhaven and smack into the arms of a rescue party, when he realised that the islander was carrying one of the sharp bone-tipped hunting spears.

Cleyton was numb and frozen, as well as being badly hampered by his thick furs which had now doubled in weight with wet, clinging snow. He tried to avoid the quick, savage blow as the Lapp islander used his spear as a staff but he was much too slow. The haft of the spear caught the side of his head and knocked him sprawling on to the snow. The ringing crack should have knocked him senseless but a lot of the blow was absorbed by the thick fur of his parka and he lay there dazed. He was on his back and somehow the torch had still remained tightly clasped in his hand, its beam pointing up at an angle into the howling blackness of the night. He saw the hooded figure in furs looming over him again, caught in the grey glow of the torch with the black hell of the blizzard raging behind him. The man stood with his feet apart and his body braced, his face covered and his eyes hidden behind protective snow goggles. He gripped the hunting spear in both hands and strained his shapeless body into the storm to steady himself as he aimed to lunge at Cleyton's throat. Despite a flurry of snow that practically smothered Cleyton's face the razor-edged bone tip of the hunting spear showed up clearly in the feeble torch light.

The wind gave its banshee howl, a shrieking cackle of deathly glee. The night was hideous with the blizzard's roar and Cleyton passed out from the pain in his head with the spear only inches from his throat.

2

A Job for Simon Larren

The green neon lizard above the doorway of the Iguana nightclub was winking its one bright red eye repeatedly at the deserted street as the West End of London approached the end of its nightly cycle of noise and gaiety. A hundred yards away a last defiant reveller was then in the process of being arrested for attempting to climb the statue of Eros in Piccadilly Circus, and only a few late-night taxis patrolled the main streets. Inside the Iguana the last cabaret performance had finished half an hour before, and Simon Larren was collecting his coat from the cloakroom.

Marylin Cross rejoined him a few moments later from the direction of the ladies cloakroom, now wearing a dark red full-length coat above her evening dress. She put her arm automatically round his waist and snuggled close to his side as he bade a calm good night to an envious doorman.

The night air struck them with a cold chill as they walked briskly away from the night-club and Larren led her directly to his pure white MG sports that stood beside a parking meter in a nearby side-street. He helped her into the low passenger seat and then quickly circled round the sleek white bonnet to the other side. He had barely closed the door before she was pulling him close again and her lips were infinitely soft as he raised them to be kissed.

At last he disentangled himself and started the engine. As the car purred into motion and he slipped it into gear, Marylin was gently tickling the inside of his left ear lobe with her little finger.

"Where are we going now?" She asked in the kind of softly contented voice that already knows the answer.

Larren had already turned the car out on to Regent Street and was heading north.

"My flat," he said calmly. "Where else?"

Marylin smiled and allowed her head to fall to one side and rest on his shoulder, her soft blonde hair brushing against his throat. She unfastened the large buttons of her coat so that he could slip one arm inside to encircle her slim waist and generally made herself comfortable. Larren's mouth registered a slight smile and he concentrated on the road.

He turned left into the wide, brightly-lit length of Oxford Street. The richly dressed plate-glass windows cruised smoothly past on either side and there were still lights high above in the top-floor windows of some of the taller office blocks. A lone constable moved at stolid regulation pace along the otherwise empty pavement and there was very little traffic. Larren felt Marylin's hand close over his own where it spread around her waist, and then she moved his hand upwards to press it firmly against her breast. He could feel the desire-hardened point of her nipple pressing through the material of her dress against his palm and looked down slowly. Marylin smiled up at him, somehow contriving to make her wide, blue eyes appear naïve and innocent. She rubbed his hand gently against her and almost automatically his foot rested more heavily upon the accelerator and the needle on the speedometer dial flickered well past the legal limit.

He turned off Oxford Street and a few minutes later the needle dipped back below the speed limit again as he entered Rushlake Terrace. He braked the sports car smoothly to a stop outside the four broad steps leading up to number twelve and deftly shut down the engine. Marylin murmured his name in a dreamy whisper and this time tickled her tongue in his ear. Larren decided to leave the side-lights burning rather than waste time driving the car round to the garages behind the haughty, Victorian-styled houses that had now been transformed into neat flats.

He disentangled himself for the second time, told her to button her coat up before she caught cold, and then hurried round to the other side of the car to help her out. She shivered as she stepped out on to the cold pavement, and Larren closed the door with a sharp thrust of his foot and practically ran her up the steps and through the glass-fronted door into the hall.

They moved more sedately up the staircase now that they had shut the sharp night air behind them and Larren led the way along the short second-floor corridor to his rooms. He unlocked the door, reached one hand inside to press down the light switch and then ushered Marylin in ahead of him. She smiled up at him as she passed, impressed by his manners, but it was not the desire to be polite that caused him to stand aside while she entered but simply the trained caution of long experience. Simon Larren had long since learned to be wary of walking first through any doorway, even in the supposed safety of his own home. He had once walked through this very same door and found himself looking straight into the ugly, bulbous eye of a silenced automatic.

The flat was comfortably furnished and Larren had left one electric fire burning so that it was already pleasantly warm. Now he switched on a second

16

fire to provide another welcome glow. A thoughtfully placed tray of bottles, glasses and a soda-water syphon stood upon a low coffee table, and two or three pre-selected records were all ready to be dropped on to the turntable of the large oak-pannelled radiogram.

Marylin looked around appreciatively and then turned to face Larren as he took off his coat and dropped it across the back of one of the two big armchairs.

"You think of everything," she said demurely.

Larren came forward and helped her out of her dark red coat, placing it on top of his own.

"I was once a boy scout," he said. "All I ever learned was the motto — be prepared."

Marylin smiled, making an attractive shrugging movement of her shoulders that were now smoothly bare above a low-cut evening dress of salmon pink. "I was never in the boy scouts," she said. "But I'm prepared too."

She waited expectantly. Larren regarded her for a moment, his gaze assessing the smooth curve of her hips and the inviting stance, and then moving up to meet the level blue of her dark-lashed eyes. Then he reached out to plant one hand firmly on each of her hips and drew her against him.

Her eager body arched slightly backwards from the waist as her arms fastened about his shoulders and her mouth trembled helplessly under his own. Her body moulded shamelessly against his and her lips parted in a low moan. For a moment she was completely submissive, and then she responded by answering the fierce pressure of his mouth and tightening her arms about him with all her strength.

After several minutes Larren raised his head and remarked calmly. "Music and liquor should have been part of the seduction treatment. Do you want a drink first?"

Marylin pulled his tie away from his neck. "Damn the drink," she said huskily. "I want you."

Larren pushed her arms down, took off his jacket and threw it on top of their coats. Then he pulled her back, kissed her again and searched for the zip fastener at the back of her dress. He found it and pulled it slowly down the length of her spine, feeling the two sides of the dress peel neatly away from the smooth bare skin of her back. Marylin continued to kiss him and at the same time her fingers fumbled at the buttons of his shirt. In that moment they both heard the sharp tap of knuckles on the door.

Larren swore softly. Marylin drew back a little and looked up into his face.

The knock on the door was repeated and reluctantly Larren zipped the pink dress half-way up again. "Take your coat and slip into the bedroom," he said quietly. "I'll see who it is."

Marylin hesitated. "All right, but get rid of them quickly, darling."

Larren nodded and handed her her coat. He ushered her into the bedroom and closed the door behind her. Then he stared speculatively at the door across the room. He was expecting no one, and at the moment he wasn't mixed up in anything that was liable to generate hostile visitors in the middle of the night. Besides, such visitors didn't usually knock. He hesitated a fraction of a second longer and then crossed over to the door. He switched off the light, knowing better than to be caught with his back to a bright background, and stood guardedly to one side as he opened the door.

A woman stood in the corridor outside, a small elderly woman wearing a man's dressing-gown several sizes too large for her over her night clothes. Larren's caution vanished as he recognised the caretaker's wife from the floor below.

"What is it, Mrs. Morgan?"

The woman shivered and huddled herself closer into what was obviously her husband's dressing-gown. "A message for you, Mr. Larren, sir. Your telephone kept ringing so many times during the evening that I took the liberty of using Morgan's key to get in and answer it. A Mr. Smith it was. He said I was to tell you that he wants to see you the moment that you came in. Terribly, terribly urgent he said it was."

Larren's stomach muscles contracted

imperceptibly, but nothing of his feelings showed on his face. He thanked the fussy little Welsh woman and evaded her curiosity with an earnest concern for her welfare and the insistence that she hurry back to her bed quickly before she caught cold. It was, he assured her, very good of her to get out of bed with the message when she heard his car arrive and he greatly appreciated it. When she had gone he went back into his room and closed the door. His unsmiling mouth had taken on a hard line and he was very still and silent in the faint red glow from the two electric fires.

A call from Smith could only mean that something big had come up. And an urgent call in the middle of the night could only mean that it was something very big. He swore softly as he realised that he would have to get rid of Marylin Cross and get over there right away.

Abruptly he moved across the dimly-lit room and opened the bedroom door. His face was determined, but when he flicked on the bedroom light his determination faltered. Marylin had removed her shoes

21

and her dress without waiting, and now she lay back hopefully on his bed wearing only her stockings, a black silk suspender belt and the tiniest pair of black lace panties he had ever seen.

She pouted her lips at him coyly and said, "Well I'm not going to do all the work. You'll have to take the rest off yourself."

Larren drew a breath and decided that the cost of a night at the Iguana club, a four-course meal with wine and a long succession of coffees and brandies was far too much to write off as a loss. Smith must have been waiting for him for most of the night, and now he could damned well wait another three minutes.

★ ★ ★

Twelve minutes later Larren was back behind the wheel of his white MG and heading fast down Oxford Street. He retraced his route down Regent Street, cut across Piccadilly Circus and turned down Haymarket towards Whitehall. Marylin Cross had been tricky to handle when he had started to get dressed again immediately after making love to her, and she had been indignantly disappointed when he explained that he had to make an urgent telephone call in answer to Mrs. Morgan's message. What she would have said had she realised that he was not coming back he hardly dared imagine, for a call from Smith meant that he could be on the next fast plane to anywhere within an hour. He had tucked her briskly into bed, closed the bedroom door on her, and swiftly scribbled a quick message of apology which he placed beneath one of the glasses on the cocktail tray. Considering himself fortunate that she had not noticed the telephone in the corner of the living-room he had then grabbed his coat and hurried out to the car.

Now he was sourly cursing Smith, whatever crisis had motivated his summons, and the whole counter-espionage department in general. He knew that as soon as Marylin found his note she would be hotly furious and that he could write off their short affair as finished. It was true that he had only regarded it as a short affair anyway, but he had been enjoying it all the same.

However, the cursing process only lasted as far as Trafalgar Square. Since the violent death of his wife several years ago Larren's life had consisted of a series of dubious missions and casual women. He did not believe himself capable of deeply loving another woman in the way that he had loved Andrea, and so he had allowed himself to be absorbed into Smith's machine. Now he relied on women who could forget quickly without being hurt, for he had no right to risk the happiness of any other kind. Marylin Cross would be furiously angry, but that was all, she would soon find comfort somewhere else. Larren had forcibly dismissed her from his mind by the time he reached Whitehall, and was already turning over a dozen possible reasons for his summons.

When he was shown into the large office that Smith inhabited in one of the ministry buildings the man himself was standing with his back to his massive desk and staring at a large map of Europe on the only wall that wasn't lined with books. He turned to face the door as Larren came in, a short, stubby, nondescript little man who aptly fitted his nondescript name. He wore a neat pin-stripe suit, a white collar and a dark-blue tie, and on the rare occasions that he left his office he donned a pompous little bowler and carried a rolled umbrella and leather brief-case that hid him among the rush-hour crowds as effectively as a grain of sand in the Sahara desert. His whole appearance built a picture of every-day meekness and servility that was abruptly shattered when he applied the cutting gaze of his clear, grey eyes the way he was looking at Larren now. The eyes were the only chink in his self-adopted guise.

He said calmly, "You took a damned long time getting here, Larren. Whose bed was it this time?" Then before Larren could answer he went on, "Not that it matters. I've got a job that looks as though it might need your special touch."

Larren remained silent. Anyone attempting to assess his character on the peculiar brooding quality of his grey-green eyes might easily have come to the conclusion that here was a man who liked to kill. And they would have been right. Larren had been trained in the gentle art of sudden death as a wartime agent of S.O.E., and he had proved a natural killer. Smith always referred to his satisfaction in tracking down and eliminating an enemy as dangerous as himself as his "special touch".

Smith beckoned him closer to the wall map. "How is your geography on the North Cape of Norway?" he asked.

"I know that there is a North Cape of Norway," Larren admitted guardedly.

"Don't worry about it," Smith advised. "You'll learn a lot more when you get there. The cold will tone your system up and you'll be able to give much better service to the tearful little maiden you undoubtedly had to leave behind."

Larren doubted very much whether his system needed toning up, he was ninety-five per cent certain that Marylin

Cross would be anything but tearful and he knew for a fact that she was most definitely no longer a maid. But Smith's face had taken on a strictly business-like look and he disdained to argue.

Smith had picked up a long pointer and was touching the map at the top of the European land mass where a short red line marked the brief Norwegian frontier with Soviet Russia. The tip of the pointer moved upwards a fraction into the Barents Sea to rest between two minute specks of land. Smith said briskly:

"As you can see the whole coast of Norway is cut with fiords and sprinkled with islands, rather like the coastline of Scotland. Well here we have two islands within half a dozen miles of each other just above the mouth of Varanger Fiord where Norway borders with Russia. One of them, Dog Island, is Norwegian; the other, Barren Island, is Soviet territory. Just lately we've had some funny reports about Barren Island, the Russians appear to have installed something there but we don't know what. One of the Lapp

Eskimos from Dog Island vanished on a hunting trip there, and then we heard that a submarine had been seen in the straits between the two. We received the reports from our opposite numbers in the Norwegian Intelligence Department. At the moment we've got two nuclear submarines and two conventional submarines doing a series of deep-Arctic tests near that region, and the Norwegians have some vague theory that the Russians may be erecting some kind of spy site on Barren Island to note the results. God knows how — or what good it will do them. However, we still want to know what is going on, so I asked for permission to put an agent on Dog Island. That agent vanished completely twenty-four hours ago."

There was a moment's silence as Smith lowered his pointer and turned to face Larren, then Larren said quietly:

"What kind of spy site could the Russians be building up there?"

Smith shrugged. "I'm damned if I know. It probably isn't anything of the kind. It was just a hazarded explanation from someone in Norwegian Intelligence because our Navy happen to be playing games near that particular area at this particular time. If anything at all it's most probably some kind of weather or research station that they're building. We've all got them scattered over the Arctic. I checked it because of the disappearance of the Eskimo, a fellow called Tunkut who went out to hunt walrus on Barren Island and didn't come back. I expected a negative report, because he could easily have had some kind of accident and either drowned or frozen to death, but now that my own man appears to have followed him I've got to take a more serious view."

Larren grimaced. "What do you know about our man's disappearance?"

"Very little. He was caught out in a blizzard and didn't return." Smith held up his hand as he saw the question forming on Larren's lips. "All right, Larren. I know he could quite easily have lost himself if there was a blizzard blowing. But when a chain of *possibly* coincidental incidents and *possibly* genuine accidents gets too long, then I start looking around for a more substantial explanation. I want one now."

"All right. The Russians are building a submarine base on Barren. Similar to those they already have on their own Arctic coastline. Similar to ours at Holy Loch. Good enough?"

"No, Larren, it's not good enough. It's too obvious and I like to look behind the obvious."

"So what do we know about these Naval exercises of our own?"

"The Admiralty says that they're just routine. The nuclear subs are doing the diving and deep-water manoeuvring tests, while the remaining two are just playing nursemaids. Despite the suggestion from the Norwegians it seems highly unlikely that they have anything at all to do with the Russian movements on Barren."

Larren took another look at the large map of Norway and the Arctic Sea and then asked the final question.

"Who was the agent who vanished on Dog Island?"

Smith said flatly, "One of my best

operatives, a man I rate higher than you. You may remember him. It was Adrian Cleyton."

Larren looked up sharply and barely checked the fractional tightening of his mouth. He remembered Cleyton well. The slim, deceptive young man with the ballet-dancer figure had twice saved his life during an exceptionally dangerous mission in the Aegean.

Smith went on. "The only possible cover I could provide was about as flimsy as you can get. Cleyton went to Dog Island as a naturalist, laden down with cameras and tape recorders for the outward purpose of filming the walrus and the Lapps. The story was weak, but if any man could have got away with it then it would have been Cleyton. Apart from an almost insipid appearance he had enough charm to convince a Belsen inmate that Hitler was a saint. The man was a born actor and could practically sell Tower Bridge to a London psychiatrist. Besides which he had a flair for languages; Greek, Russian, Norwegian and two or three others."

He paused and then said grimly, "But it seems that not even Cleyton could get away with it this time. Someone removed him from the picture. And that means that it's useless to send in another agent who relies on subtlety. The other side are playing rough, and for keeps, so the only thing that I can do is to send out a man who plays the same way. Cleyton was a top-line agent, but he was no ruthless killer — you are, Larren, and you're the man who is going to take his place."

He smiled with sudden benevolence. "I hope you've already bought your woolly winter underwear, Larren. It's rather cold up there in the Arctic."

3

Crash Landing

Larren turned away from the wall map and sat down in one of the two easy chairs which, apart from the massive desk, comprised the whole furniture of the book-lined office. He looked into Smith's fathomless grey eyes and accepted the little man's silence as an invitation to speak.

"You've already made it plain that no cover on earth can protect the next agent to appear on Dog Island — so how exactly do I arrive? Charging up the beach in my long winter underwear, waving the Union Jack and shouting British Bulldog and Rule Britannia until all the nasty Russians run away? Because if so I have a horrible feeling that the Russians may not be impressed."

Smith fixed him with a hard stare. "Am I to understand that you are declining to volunteer for the job?"

Larren smiled. "Not exactly, but I am wondering whether you have any better ideas?"

"As a matter of fact I have." Smith didn't smile. He crossed over to his desk and buzzed for his secretary, then he said curtly, "Send Carver in now, Miss Westerham."

He straightened up from the desk and waited, and almost immediately the door was opened and Larren heard the quiet, unhurried voice of Smith's secretary announcing Mr. Carver. Larren twisted in his chair to get a better look at the newcomer and then Smith said:

"Larren, meet Joe Carver. He's the man who is going to put you down on Dog Island."

Larren didn't blink as the big, black-haired man limped towards him, but he was startled none the less. The men who worked for Smith rarely looked the part, but Joe Carver was in a class of his own. Apart from the limp in his left leg his whole face was a scarred mess of burns and unsuccessful attempts at plastic surgery. He stopped a few paces in front of Larren and smiled faintly. The smile revealed a hint of even white teeth and suggested that the ravaged face must once have been handsome. He said calmly:

"You don't flinch easily, Larren. I'm glad of that. Because when you hear how I intend to put you down on Dog Island you'll probably consider that you have good reason to do more than flinch."

Larren looked at Smith. "This sounds healthier every minute."

Smith retreated behind his desk but did not sit down. He said bluntly, "A few years ago Joe Carver was the best stunt man in the British film industry. Every time an aeroplane crashed on the screen, or a motor boat blew up or a car dived over a cliff, Joe was at the wheel. Crashes were his speciality — anything from rolling sports cars off the M.1. to staging head-on collisions in mid-air. Then came the crash he almost didn't survive. The one that ended his career. Because no amount of make-up could cover those scars to allow him to continue doubling for smooth-faced film stars. But he can still stage a crash better than any man alive, and now he's going to stage one for you."

Smith abruptly decided to sit down and then continued, "Joe is going to take off on a routine flight from Norway to parachute supplies to a weather research station on the polar ice cap. You, Larren, will be flying with him as co-pilot. *En route* Joe will deliberately fly off course, feign engine trouble, and crash-land on Dog Island."

This time Larren did blink. "Delightful," he said at last. "Utterly delightful."

Smith ignored him. "There is a small settlement on the island. It's called Stadhaven. There's nothing much there except a handful of Lapp Eskimoes who live by fishing and hunting walrus. However, there is a Norwegian doctor up there — a woman — a doctor Margaret Norstadt. She flew up there towards the end of the summer to handle a flu epidemic that killed off several of the islanders. When the outbreak occurred she was the nearest doctor available and volunteered without hesitation. The crisis is over now and there's a boat due to take her off in about seven days' time. She's staying on until the last minute before the Arctic night fully sets in for the sake of a few stragglers who are still recovering, so she'll still be there when you arrive.

"Now to cope voluntarily with a flu epidemic on an Arctic island means that Margaret Norstadt is a pretty resourceful woman, definitely not the shrinking-violet type. When she hears the crash it's certain that she'll send out a rescue party — or even lead it. You two men will feign injury until that party arrives and allow yourselves to be carried back to Stadhaven. The doctor won't be able to examine you at all until she gets you inside somewhere, because to remove your furs out in the open will expose you to severe frost-bite and probably kill you. When she does get round to examining you is when you will have to take her into your confidence, for you'll need her help to maintain the pretence that you're both too seriously injured to be moved. What line of action you'll take from there I don't know. But that, Larren, is your problem. Joe's job is to get you on to that island without the other side being one hundred per cent certain that you are Cleyton's replacement. Even this way they'll be suspicious, but it should give you a couple of days' grace."

Carver's faint smile appeared again. "Don't worry, the crash will look good. If a crash has Joe Carver's name on it then it's guaranteed."

"Maybe." Larren was still dubious. "But after that everything is going to hinge on the co-operation of this Norstadt woman. And she looks to be in too convenient a position at a too convenient time. How can we be sure that she isn't already mixed up in the whole affair?"

Smith said grimly. "I'd trade quite a lot to be sure about Margaret Norstadt. I've checked with the Norwegians and they've verified that she is exactly what she claims to be, but she could be all of that and still have been suborned by the Reds. There's absolutely no record of her having ever been in contact with any known Communist influence, but in the cases of the really clever ones there never is. Margaret Norstadt is a gamble that we've just got to take, because there's no other way."

Larren didn't like the idea one little bit, but he refrained from saying so.

Smith went on, "What I want, Larren, are the facts behind the Russian activity on Barren Island. I also want to know why that Eskimo hunter vanished, and what happened to Adrian Cleyton. In the remote likelihood of Cleyton being still alive bring him back if you can, but not if it means endangering your own safety, or Carver's, or the fulfilment of the main job. Cleyton knew the score when he went out there, exactly the same as everybody else."

Larren's face was expressionless, but he owed a debt to Adrian Cleyton, and if the slim man was dead then the ugly flicker in Larren's grey-green eyes boded ill for the man or men responsible.

★ ★ ★

The twin props of the ex-wartime R.A.F. Blenheim's two 840 h.p. air-cooled radial engines droned steadily through grey skies and trailing shreds of tattered cloud. The plane's speed was just under two hundred miles per hour and she was flying at four thousand feet. The ice-coated mountains and freezing fiords of Norway appeared briefly and then vanished again through the occasional gaps in the muck below. Farther south there had been vast snow-covered pine forests, but here the few patches of earth that passed into momentary visibility were barren and inhospitable, cold and empty. They had flown slightly inland shortly after crossing the Arctic circle, leaving the fantastically carved and scattered, ice-glittering coastline behind them as they entered thickening cloud. Now they were beginning to appreciate the savage bite of the northern winter. It was fourteen hours since the unassuming Mr. Smith had issued his orders, and the last of the day's light was beginning to fade into increasing greyness.

Simon Larren had to suppress a shiver, despite the fact that he was dressed in the best possible Arctic clothing, from nylon-stringed, heat-retaining underwear to his thick outer furs, and he turned his gaze slowly from the already frosted window to the interior of the Blenheim's cabin where Joe Carver sat beside him at the controls. Carver too was padded out with bulky furs and he was navigating on instruments alone, flying blind into the murk. The ex stunt-man's ravaged face had a ghastly, unearthly look in the faint green glow that came from some of the dials on the instrument panel in front of him. The ghostly light illuminated the burn scars across the lower half of his face, and heightened the edges of a skin graft that had not healed perfectly across his forehead.

Carver sensed Larren's shiver and glanced around. He smiled, faintly as always. Perhaps he had long ago realised that to smile too broadly would only increase the ugly twists in his cheeks.

"Cold, Larren? Or is my face beginning to disturb you?"

"A combination of both. How did it happen?"

Carver shrugged. "It was a car crash — a

scene for a film called *Death Drivers*. The scene was the climax of the picture and called for a car to race down a side road in an effort to intercept a petrol lorry coming down the main highway. It ended in a dead heat and a glorious collision, everything going up in one crashing sheet of flame. I drove the car, another stunt man drove the lorry. It should have been quite simple because we were both fully experienced at rolling out of a fast-moving car on the camera's blind side at the last minute. The other driver did a perfect job. But I was a bloody perfectionist. I left it to the last minute and then caught the turn-up of my trouser leg on the accelerator as I twisted to open the door. I was still in the car when it hit."

Carver drew a deep breath. "Can you picture it, Larren? The car hit and the petrol lorry exploded — just as the producer wanted it. Simultaneously my leg broke and I was catapulted out of the already-opened door. In the split-second before the impact I clapped one hand over my eyes, and only that saved me

42

from being blinded. As it was I was shot through a sheet of flaming petrol that burned every strip of flesh off my face and the back of my hand."

Larren shivered, and this time it wasn't the cold. "You should be dead."

Carver nodded. "I would have been but for two things. One was that I was wearing a very effective asbestos suit beneath my jacket and trousers, and two was that we had a fully-equipped fire-fighting unit standing by. They pulled me clear in a matter of seconds."

Carver fell silent in the eerie glow from the panel. The Blenheim droned on, the blurr of her props barely visible through the cabin windows. Larren thought Carver was reluctant to recall any more of his ordeal and was prepared to let the subject drop, but after a few minutes the big man went on:

"I spent quite a while in hospital after that. My left leg had snapped in three places when I was thrown out of that car, and although the doctors did a pretty good job of sticking it together again it got a little twisted and lost a couple of inches in the process. With my face they had even less success. They had to wait a long time for the flesh to grow on my face again, and even then I proved to have a poor response to plastic surgery. I had three operations before they could let me out of hospital and I've been back for several since. Now I've just about given up hope."

Larren said slowly, "How did you get mixed up in this business?"

Carver smiled again, more faintly than ever. "I suppose you could call it a kind of natural progress. The first thing I did on leaving hospital was to go back to the film studio and crash another car. I've had broken bones before and I wasn't going to let this little lot stop me. But I hadn't reckoned on the state of my face. I couldn't double for the big stars any more, except in long shots when the camera couldn't pick out my face. And it didn't take long before I faced up to the fact that I was finished in the film business. It was soon after that that I encountered Smith. Indirectly, of course. He needed a diversion outside an office block in West Berlin. I provided it by ramming a Volkswagen into a wall. After that Smith found it quite useful to have an expert stunt man on call. I executed quite a few diversions and fake accidents, though I must admit that this is the first time I've been asked to crash-land a plane in the Arctic."

Larren said seriously. "What exactly are our chances?"

"Pretty good. Dog Island is reasonably flat, snow-cushioned, and provided there isn't a blizzard raging we should make it okay."

Larren decided not to dwell upon the prospect and switched the subject. "You must find life pretty dull after moving in film circles."

"That's so." Carver looked at him slowly and his faint smile was definitely bitter. "You may not believe it, Larren, but I was a good-looking guy before I ploughed into that petrol lorry. In the film business there were plenty of women around, eager young girls all grabbing for star parts. And quite a lot of them went in a big way for Joe Carver. A kind of hero-worship I suppose. I could match the top-name lover boys in the beauty stakes, and on top of that I was out there doing the dangerous jobs while they were having their hair permed in the make-up room. That's how it looked to a lot of the girls anyway. Before the crash I was living high wide and handsome.

"Afterwards of course it was all finished. I was still a top stunt man, but the guys on the body odour adverts had nothing on me when it came to turning the women away. It was that that I really couldn't take. I needed the tricky, unrehearsed jobs that only Smith could provide to create a new challenge in life. Now I kind of like it. I still get a bit sour sometimes. But I had enough women in my heyday to last most men a lifetime. So now I get philosophic."

Carver relapsed into silence again, concentrating on his instruments, and Larren refrained from probing any deeper. It was several hours now since they had stopped to rest and refuel at Trondheim before crossing the Arctic circle and now there was total darkness outside the faint glow from the Blenheim's cabin. The weather was worsening and ice was beginning to form on the wing-tips. A strong cross-wind was beginning to blow from the west, and although Larren had been expecting it he could not suppress the cold feeling of apprehension that gripped him as the heavy gusts buffeted the perspex windows of the cabin. Carver remained unmoved. The weather report was one of the factors that had caused Carver to cut short their stay at Trondheim and get underway again. He could blame the storm force winds for blowing him off his supposed course and carrying him towards Dog Island.

Larren had not been too happy with the decision, for the early take-off meant a night arrival at the lonely Arctic island and a crash-landing in pitch darkness. But Carver had pointed out that to arrive in broad daylight and calm weather was going to make their accidental landing look pretty weak, and at this stage Carver called the tune. Larren could only trust his judgement. He knew that Carver was an excellent pilot with long hours of wartime flying in Blenheims — that was one of the reasons why Smith had secured a Blenheim, the other was because it was an old plane and they were going to crash it anyway — and he had to take it for granted that Carver knew what he was doing.

Another hour droned by, and then it began to snow. The storm had gained force and the quick flurries of white flakes that flashed up from the dark sky began to spatter violently across the windscreen like streams of white tracer fire. The Blenheim dropped through an air pocket with a sudden jolt that made Larren tighten his mouth while Carver smiled briefly. The storm lashed the old fighter-bomber across the ugly sky and ice-spikes of hail showered the fuselage.

Carver said calmly, "I'd try climbing, but we should be nearing Varanger fiord and the open sea, and I've got to spot the lights of Kirkenes on the edge of the fiord to get a final navigation fix."

Larren said nothing, staring grimly out of the window as Carver pushed the stick forward to start the Blenheim's nose dropping lower through the sky. The snow continued to drift up against the windscreen. Larren could barely see their own props and he wondered how the hell Carver expected to see the lights of the town below.

Carver continued to keep the stick forward, watching the altitude dial with steady blue eyes. The needle on the dial dropped gradually from four to one thousand feet and still they were in the storm.

At five hundred feet the Blenheim sank below the level of the full force winds, but continued to descend through the falling snow that whipped across the cockpit. The plane was becoming sluggish and Carver remarked almost conversationally that the ice was probably lying heavy on the wings. And then at three hundred feet the scar-faced pilot gave a satisfied grunt and referred quickly to the navigation pad strapped to his knee. Larren peered downwards and could just distinguish the dim suggestion of scattered lights through the swirling snow. Carver drew the stick back until the Blenheim levelled out and headed her a few degrees east of north. "Not bad," he said. "I was afraid my navigation might have been just a little bit rusty."

Larren grimaced. "Now you tell me."

Fifteen minutes later they were out over the Barents Sea and flying low at a hundred feet. Both men were peering through the grey-black murk of snow and darkness and Carver was inching the plane lower towards the unseen wave-tops. At this height they entered a pocket of twisting cross-winds that jockeyed the plane in nerve-wracking drops and bumps and caused Carver to frown grimly. If the twisted expression on his face was a frown.

Larren's eyes ached but still he could see nothing, and now he began to breathe a little more heavily as a touch of fear wriggled through his stomach. They had relied upon the wind direction to help substantiate their story of being blown off course in the minds of the men on Barren Island whom they ultimately expected it to reach, but now he realised that the wind could quite easily and ironically force them off their true course and plunge them straight into the freezing death of the Arctic seas.

Then at fifty feet Carver uttered a violent exclamation and heaved on the stick. The Blenheim's nose jerked upwards and she climbed rapidly.

"Wave tops," Carver explained tersely. "Thirty feet below us. But there's land directly ahead. I caught a glimpse of breakers pounding the ice floes. We're going down again."

Larren, who had seen nothing, was beginning to realise that Carver's night-sight was much keener than his own, and felt slightly reassured. Carver dipped the stick again and the Blenheim lost height, and almost immediately Larren saw and heard the crashing of broken ice slabs rearing up that Carver had seen before. But it was only a glimpse, directly below them, and then it was gone.

The Blenheim levelled out and Carver leaned forward on his seat. His gloved hand moved to the switches on the control panel and instantly the port engine lost its steady purr and began to splutter violently. Carver moved the switch a second time and the engine swiftly regained its former note. Carver glanced at Larren and smiled.

"Local colour, we've got to make it sound as though we're really in trouble."

He cut the engine again and allowed it to cough and splutter once more. Each time he juggled the switches the spinning blur of the propeller almost stopped and the plane sagged lower through the sky. He pulled the stick and climbed to gain more height and then banked the Blenheim in a staggering circle, again flicking the motor on and off.

Larren could only hope that the island actually was underneath them as Carver allowed the plane to reel drunkenly round, for he had seen nothing apart from that one glimpse of sea-pounded ice. He felt blind and helpless in the wildly-rocking plane and had to trust implicitly in Carver's more finely-adjusted night-sight. And then, after a complete circle, Carver pushed the stick slowly forward and murmured:

"Hold tight! This is it."

The faint smile was again evident on Carver's face as the tiny cabin angled down and forward, and he calmly switched off the port engine for the last time. The propeller stopped with a final vibrant shudder, and then the plane was swooping down out of the black, storm-filled sky, the one remaining prop on the starboard engine whirring through sheets of snow. And in that moment Larren thought of a dozen things that could go drastically wrong.

They could be landing on the wrong island, in which case the only rescue party they could expect would consist of armed Soviet soldiers. Or they could over-shoot and still crash into the below-zero seas. And even if Carver's navigation was spot-on there was still a vast difference between crashing a plane to order on a well-surveyed film location and doing the same thing on an unknown speck of Arctic land in the middle of a night snowstorm.

Then, with terrifying suddenness, the Blenheim crashed.

4

Doctor Margaret

Larren was braced in his seat and staring tensely through the cabin windows into the rushing nightmare of snow and darkness ahead, but still he saw nothing to indicate that they were nearing the ground until the actual moment of impact. The plane hit down, bounced violently and was slammed down again by the storm in a shattering series of jolts that rattled his teeth together and seemed as though it must rip his re-straining harness straps through his body like cutting wires through cheese. The plane bounced a second time, crashed down and skidded across ice and snow like a wild thing, maddened by wind and night. Carver was fighting desperately with the control column in an effort to stop her kicking up again and his scarred face was bestially twisted as he clenched his teeth in the green glow from the panel. The plane heeled over to one side and the dipping wing-tip scooped up a spraying cloud of frozen snow. Larren's chest was bursting from the crushing pressure of his safety straps and then abruptly the skidding plane rammed into some solid obstacle and the strap across Larren's left shoulder tore away from the seat behind him. Larren was flung forward and his head hit the cabin window with a terrific impact that seemed to smash its way clear inside his skull. The blow knocked him unconscious but in the instant that it happened he seemed to hear Joe Carver cry out in agony. The Blenheim had come to rest against a hump-backed ridge of snow and ice and there she stayed. Silence settled inside the small cabin, and outside the wind howled and the drifting snow piled up against the fuselage.

★ ★ ★

Larren returned slowly from darkness and choked on the raw brandy that was trickling down his throat. Consciousness

55

began to rush back at him and he swallowed involuntarily, coughing helplessly as he did so. The brandy fired new life into his stomach and made him realise that he was aching all over. The pain in his head was enough to make him want to scream and when he tightened his mouth against it he could taste blood on his lips. He was dimly aware that it was bitterly cold.

With an effort he opened his eyes. He was still in the cabin of the Blenheim, but now the sliding roof above his head was open and the snow was swirling inside. There was a whining, roaring sound that he took a long time to associate with the winds battering the plane's sides, but the main fact that registered was the fact that he was looking into the most magnificent pair of silver-grey eyes that he had ever seen.

The eyes looked at him from the deep fur hood of a parka and the rest of the face was hidden by a protective mask and raised snow goggles pushed up on to the temples. But they were definitely a woman's eyes. No man could have possessed eyes as beautiful as that.

The scene registered for a moment and then he had to close his eyes against the drumming in his head. A gloved finger and thumb applied gentle pressure to the corners of his tightened lips, forcing his mouth slightly open, and then another trickle of brandy burned its way over his tongue. This time he was able to swallow without choking.

When he could see again the silver-grey eyes were still there, but now she had pulled the face mask down and was speaking quietly.

"Don't move anything. Just relax and tell me if you feel any pain at all apart from the cut across your head?"

Larren tried to free his mind from the one dominating pain and realised slowly that apart from the general feeling of being bruised all over the rest of his body appeared to be undamaged. But he remembered Smith's orders to feign injury until he could speak to Margaret Norstadt alone, and now he could hear other voices outside the plane.

He said weakly, "I think my ribs are

cracked. I'm not sure of anything else."

He remembered Joe Carver for the first time and despite the flood of agony that it caused he twisted his head to one side. Carver was slumped forward limply in his seat, his body held in position by his harness. A spasm of alarm moved through Larren's body, and then he realised that Carver too was acting on Smith's orders to feign injury. Carver was too much of an expert to be hurt. He looked back to Margaret Norstadt, for the fact that there was no other woman on Dog Island left no doubt of her identity.

"It's all right," she said. "He's alive. I don't know how badly he's hurt because he's still unconscious, and I can't examine him out here. I'll have to get him back to Stadhaven. You were lucky, you came down less than a mile from the one and only settlement on the island. I heard the crash and organised the Lapps to come out and get you."

There was a scratching sound on the roof of the fuselage and Larren looked upwards, the movement sent more pain shooting through his head and his face creased in agony. He was dimly aware of a second hooded figure in Arctic furs crouching above the open escape hatch, and of dark bright eyes peering down at him from a round, yellow-brown face that was again framed in a thick, flapping fur hood. And then he felt suddenly sick and the pressure of pain waves closed his eyes and forced him to cling hard to his seat. Margaret Norstadt's voice reached him faintly.

"Don't worry, we're going to get you out of here. But it could be a rough trip so we'll make things easy and send you to sleep first."

Larren was desperately fighting the urge to faint and barely heard her words, or realised what she meant to do. He sensed her stoop down in front of him, pressing against his knees in the cramped confines of the cabin, but he did not open his eyes to see her pick up the pre-prepared hypodermic syringe that lay on top of her opened first-aid kit at her feet. He felt her remove his glove and then the needle pricked deep inside his wrist. The jab made him fight more strongly and open his eyes, for it was important that he did not pass out. He saw the beautiful silver-grey eyes smiling down at him for the last time, and then her face became blurred and despite himself he was slipping back into unconsciousness. He hung on to his seat with frantic hands, but his grip lost strength and the anchoring seat was washed away from beneath him on a wave of blackness.

★ ★ ★

The trip back to Stadhaven was a rough one, but with the aid of her Eskimo helpers Margaret Norstadt made it in thirty-five minutes. Her small medical outpost on the edge of the tiny Eskimo settlement was comprised of three prefabricated huts, two of them small storehouses and the third, the long main building, containing her living quarters and the small emergency hospital that had been swiftly erected during the summer to combat the flu epidemic.

She pushed open the door and gusts of snow followed her into the narrow corridor that ran between the outer wall of the hut and the partitioned rooms. Quickly she turned to hurry up the stretcher-bearing Lapps, and once they had shuffled past her she slammed the door thankfully behind them.

She pushed past the stretcher-bearers again and directed them into the small hospital ward next to her surgery. The ward had once been full but now all the beds were empty. The Eskimos lowered their burdens to the floor and looked at her with expectant, beaming faces as she swiftly stripped off her face mask and snow goggles.

She issued brisk orders and her cheerful assistants quickly unstrapped the two men from their stretchers. They lifted Joe Carver on to the nearest of the four hospital beds, and then carried Simon Larren into the small surgery and placed him on the couch where she could stitch up the gash across his forehead. While they did so the doctor stripped off her heavy outer furs and then moved over to thaw her hands in the heat from the large oil stove that was kept continually burning. She warmed them only briefly and then rubbed them furiously together, screwing up her face against the exquisite pain that came as the circulation prickled like a red-hot electric current through her frozen fingers.

The Lapps came out of the surgery and stood in a circle watching her, black-eyed curious little men who never stopped smiling. They looked like squat puff-balls of shaggy fur, topped by wrinkled yellow-brown faces and stiff black hair where they had pushed back their huge fur hoods. She smiled in turn and thanked them as well as she was able for their help. They seemed slightly disappointed that it was all over and their curiosity unsatisfied, but finally they all nodded solemnly and trooped reluctantly out.

When they had gone she continued rubbing the life back into her hands and finally moved over to where Joe Carver lay on his back on the bed. The pilot's hood had fallen back from his face and he was still unconscious.

She saw the unappetising maze of burned scar tissue for the first time, and recoiled in sudden horror. Then she realised that they were all old scars and forced herself to move closer, bending low over the mutilated face. After a few moments she straightened up and looked down the length of the big man's bulky body, her mouth tightened a little when she saw the twisted left leg. She hesitated, and then turned away towards the surgery, for it was clear that Carver was going to remain unconscious for some time yet.

Simon Larren was already showing signs of recovery, despite the injection she had given him. He lay on his back on the surgery couch with frozen blood on the side of his face. She looked down at him and shuddered again, for in its way the hard lean face with its tight unsmiling mouth indicated a man more to be feared than Carver. There was something about both of them, even when unconscious that stamped them as men who could be both hard and ruthless, and remembering Larren's cold grey-green eyes, she felt that he would be the more dangerous.

She hesitated for a moment, and then flexed her fingers and decided that her hands were now capable of the tasks that were before them. Swiftly she began to remove Larren's outer furs, moving gently only when she peeled back the hood that had stuck to the open gash above his temple. She cleaned the jagged three-inch gash and then shaved away the hair around it before deftly stitching the edges together. She bandaged a lint pad across the wound and then carefully washed the blood from the rest of his face. He stirred as she worked and then suddenly his eyelids flickered upwards.

★ ★ ★

Larren's last thought before passing out was that he must not succumb to the doctor's knock-out injection in case she realised that neither he nor Carver were seriously hurt and revealed the information before he recovered to warn her. The thought was still with him as he felt the cotton-wool swab dabbing the blood away from his cheeks and opened his eyes.

Margaret Norstadt said quickly, "Don't move yet. I haven't had time to look at those ribs."

Larren's head was still throbbing inside as well as smarting savagely around the cut, but with an effort he ignored it.

"Don't bother about the ribs," he said weakly. "There's nothing wrong with them."

Margaret Norstadt looked at him doubtfully. She was younger than Larren had expected, not more than thirty. Now that she had got out of her furs her figure was good without being exceptional and she was wearing a high roll-necked sweater of red and orange wool that fitted close around her throat. Her hair was a ripe, primrose-yellow and slightly reminiscent of Marylin Cross. But there the resemblance ended for this capable young Norwegian woman was of a very different calibre indeed.

She said slowly, "What do you mean?"

Larren said bluntly, "I mean that

neither of us are really hurt and that that accident was a fake." He saw the professional, sanity-doubting look come into her eyes and swiftly explained. When he had finished the look was still there.

"I heard the plane circling before it crashed," she said flatly. "And I heard the motors cut out several times as the pilot had trouble with the engines."

"I know. We had to make it look good."

She glared down at him and a trace of anger crept into her voice. "Do you really mean that I've spent the last hour stumbling about outside in the freezing cold with a rescue party just for the sake of some stupid game?"

"Not for a stupid game. It was the only possible way I could get here without arousing suspicion."

"Arousing suspicion! For God's sake! Whose suspicion? There's nobody on Dog Island except a handful of Lapps and myself, and you claim that you need my co-operation."

Larren said harshly, "There's the Reds

on Barren Island."

"So what? Why should they concern themselves with what goes on here?"

"They concerned themselves enough to eliminate the last man we sent." She was looking at him blankly and he added, "I mean Cleyton."

"Cleyton? But he was just a naturalist. The fool got himself lost in a blizzard. I tried to get him to take a couple of the Lapps with him, but he would insist on going out there alone."

Larren said grimly, "You didn't know Adrian Cleyton. He was one of the best men in counter-espionage — and not the kind of man to get himself lost in an Arctic blizzard."

Margaret Norstadt said flatly, "And you don't know Arctic blizzards."

Larren sat up on the couch with an effort, wincing as the stitches pulled at his forehead. "Listen to me," he said earnestly. "You must have a radio here and in normal circumstances you'd report our crash back to your base and ask for a ship to take us off. Well do that, and include the story that we were blown off course. The Reds are sure to be listening in across the straits and picking up your messages. It's the obvious thing for them to do, and with luck they'll swallow our cover story. I don't doubt that they'll send somebody across to investigate the plane, but the wreckage will back up our story all the way, the equipment that we are supposed to be flying up to that weather station farther north is actually stowed away in parachute packs inside the fuselage. No doubt someone will also attempt to question one of your Eskimos, but they too will only be able to back up the story that we were both carried out of the plane. And if you add that Carver and myself are both suffering from broken bones and unfit to be moved in your report, then that should give me a few days' grace in which to find out what happened to Cleyton, and what the Reds are doing on Barren Island. I can operate at night and avoid the islanders."

Margaret Norstadt looked at him sceptically. "You can't seriously believe that those primitive Eskimoes are all Russian spies."

"No." Larren's patience was wearing thin. "But if anybody talks to them and asks questions then they'll tell exactly what they know. That's why Carver and I allowed you to knock us out with that injection and carry us here. I want the Eskimos to tell of what they have seen."

The young Norwegian woman still frowned.

Larren said bluntly, "I've told you the facts. Can we rely on you to help us or not?"

She hesitated a second longer and then said slowly, "It seems that I've got to believe you. I don't think you're mad and there's no other explanation. I still find it hard to believe that Cleyton was an espionage agent, but it does explain a lot of his strange behaviour. And I'm pretty sure myself that there's something very fishy going on on that Soviet island." Her silver-grey eyes regarded him for a moment and then she went on, "But your cover is better than you think if you believe that your friend is still simply feigning injury. I didn't have to give an injection to knock him out at all because he's been unconscious ever since your plane crashed. His left leg is snapped in at least two places."

5

A Shoal of Dead Fish

When they examined Carver fully Larren saw that the stuntpilot's leg was broken both above the knee and above the ankle. Both were clean breaks with no messy bones sticking through the flesh and Margaret Norstadt efficiently strapped up the limb in splints while Carver was still unconscious. As Larren watched he realised that whatever else the blonde Norwegian might be she was a good doctor. He had helped her to remove Carver's furs and when she had finished attending to the broken leg he helped her again to get the big man underneath the blankets on his bed. He stepped back out of the way while she finished making Carver comfortable and closed his eyes against the throbbing head pains that had redoubled as he had moved about.

After a moment he felt her hand on

his arm, a firm no-nonsense grip. "Come through here," she commanded. "There's nothing more we can do for your friend at the moment."

Larren saw no reason for argument and allowed her to lead him out of the hospital into a smaller room that was obviously her living quarters. The centre-piece was another large oil stove that threw out a hot, red glow faintly illuminating the rest of the room. There was a wall-cupboard full of crockery and canned foods. A primus cooking-stove, a table and a chair and a stack of medical books and lighter novels on a shelf. It would have looked spartan but for the crisp, white cloth on the table, some brightly-coloured rugs on the floor and a tasteful selection of water-colours on the wall. She steered him into the chair and Larren closed his eyes again as she busied herself with lighting the oil lamp that hung from the ceiling.

He heard her move past him and then came the clink of a bottle touching a glass. A moment later she came back and with an effort he opened his eyes to find her standing in front of him, watching him intently. She was standing with her feet slightly apart and looked a very capable young woman in her dark slacks and the bright red-and-orange sweater. She held a glass in each hand and thrust one towards him.

"You look as though you need it," she said authoritatively. Larren took the glass and tasted it. The familiar Scotch whisky burned his throat and he tried to smile. She drank half her own glass, and Larren noticed that that too was neat Scotch — medicinal, no doubt. She sat one hip on the edge of the table, still watching him, and said flatly: "Well, what are you going to do now? Neither of you are fit to carry on."

"I can carry on." Larren's voice was harsher than he meant it to be, but the ache in his head was impairing his control. "I'll need a day or so to get over the worst effects of this crack on the head, but we intended to lay low for a couple of days anyway. We want the Lapps to get used to the idea of having a couple of injured men at the hospital."

"All right." Her tone didn't alter. "But what do you intend to carry on and do?"

"You tell me. What do you think is happening on Barren Island?"

"I don't know. How should I?"

"But you know that something fishy is going on — you said as much when you agreed to help me. So what makes you think that? The disappearance of Cleyton, or the Eskimo — or what?"

She said dubiously, "It wasn't so much the disappearance of Cleyton. He was a stranger to the Arctic, and it was quite conceivable that he shouldn't come back after being caught in a blizzard. But the disappearance of Tunkut did seem strange. I know walrus hunting is dangerous and it's not unknown for them to get killed by a charging bull, but the Lapps here on Dog live solely by fishing and hunting the walrus, and Tunkut was one of the best hunters of all. He paddled across to Barren in his kayak and the weather was just about as good as it can be in this part of the world at this time of year. He left during the few hours of daylight, and simply never came back."

"Didn't his friends go and look for him?"

"Not until a few days had passed. Then when they did get concerned and started out after him something happened to start them running straight back. They said that a monster came rearing up out of the sea between here and Barren, a huge blind thing with a monstrous fin that chased them away. They claimed that as the monster had obviously eaten Tunkut then it was pointless to search for him any more."

Larren's head was pounding violently with the effort to concentrate. He said slowly, "The monster was the submarine that you reported, but did it actually chase them away?"

Margaret smiled. "Of course not, it was just the sight of it that scared them off."

"Did you actually see the submarine?"

"No, but when they described it there was nothing else that it possibly could have been. And don't ask me what it was doing there because I have no idea. It must have been coincidence that it appeared just as the Lapps were starting out on their search for Tunkut, because it's too far-fetched to imagine that it was there solely for the purpose of frightening them away. But I haven't a clue as to what its real purpose might have been."

Neither had Larren and he had to pass that question for a moment. "What else can you tell me about Barren?" he asked.

"Have you ever been there?"

She shook her head. "I've never had any reason to go there. As far as I know it's just another frozen piece of land about the same size as Dog. It's uninhabited, because most of the walrus herds are centred on Dog, but just lately there've been one or two indications that something is at least arousing interest in the island. Twice I've heard ships out there in the night. I don't know whether they were submarines or what they were, because I couldn't tell one from the other by sound alone, but I've definitely heard the engines of ships of some kind."

Larren recalled the report of a landing

stage that had been seen by the pilot of the Norwegian fisheries department plane which he had heard from Smith and asked, "Do you think the Russians are building something out there?"

"What sort of something?"

"Any sort of something!" Larren's aching head was affecting his temper and he had trouble in keeping his voice down. The doctor regarded him shrewdly and then answered his question.

"Again I don't know. I've just heard boat engines out there in the night. I have no idea what they can mean. I suppose they could be building something, but there again I have no idea what that something might be." She paused for a moment and then went on, "Anyway, Barren Island is Soviet territory, even if the Russians are using it for some unexplained purpose, what can you do about it?"

Larren said flatly, "We can find out what it is that they are doing — that's all that my job entails."

"And after that?"

"After that it's somebody else's

problem." Larren finished his glass of whisky and silently cursed the advance waves of pain that kept sweeping through his thinking. He felt that there was a lot he had missed, a lot of questions that he should have asked, but his brain was too blurred by pain.

Margaret calmly removed the glass from his hand, emptied her own, and then walked over to where the bottle stood on top of the wall-cupboard and poured two more. She came back and this time sat on the other side of the table, resting her weight on her right hip. Full, nicely-curved hips, Larren noticed, the dark slacks fitting snugly. Good child-raising hips, he thought vaguely. He accepted his filled glass and decided that there was probably a very good figure beneath that shapeswamping sweater; the thrust of the breasts was firm and prominent enough. In fact, good child-raising material all round. Despite her air of firm competence and the fact that she was no shrinking violet Margaret Norstadt was still a very desirable woman. He liked the yellow-blonde hair too. He had shown a marked preference for blondes in the later years since his beloved Andrea had died. A blonde was in complete contrast to his dead wife's auburn curls, and they never stirred the deep emptiness in his heart the way that a red-or dark-haired girl sometimes could. And there were those eyes too —

His thoughts broke off as he realised that he was staring directly into those keenly appraising silver-grey eyes.

Margaret said quietly, "I think you should rest. You're in no condition to continue the conversation."

"Later." Larren spoke the word explosively and the very violence behind it told him that she was right. He repeated more sanely, "I'll rest later. What else can you tell me about Barren Island? Was — was Cleyton going there when he vanished?"

She shook her head. "No, Cleyton was not going to Barren."

"How can you be sure? He may have borrowed a boat of some kind from the Lapps."

She said wearily, "He didn't borrow a

boat or one of them would have told me. The only boats they possess are kayaks anyway. In these seas he wouldn't have dared to use one."

Larren had to make another effort to stay calm. "I told you that Cleyton was a trained agent. He was quite capable of handling any sort of boat — even an Eskimo kayak."

"But he didn't," she said firmly. "When Cleyton left here he was heading for a small cove on the west side of the island. If you'll stop shooting questions and relax for a moment I'll show you why." She slipped off the table and straightened up. "Are you fit to walk back into the surgery?"

Larren said slowly, "I'm fit."

Despite his assurance she had to steady him as he got up from his chair and a fresh wave of pounding broke out in his skull. She led him through the small hospital ward and back into the surgery where he had first recovered consciousness.

"Wait here," she said, and then left him.

She went to a wall-cupboard and took down a small black box which she placed on the surgery desk. The box was fitted with several switches, a carrying handle and a large dial. There was a coiled extension plugged into it that looked like a roving hand microphone such as a singer might use on the stage. Larren recognised it, and for a moment he managed to forget the wound in his head as he watched the doctor's movements with narrowed eyes.

She knelt down before another wall-cupboard and drew out a square enamel bowl, the type that a lot of doctors use as a container for sterilised instruments. She straightened up and placed the bowl on the table and gestured Larren to come closer. He moved up beside her and saw that the bowl contained a fish, an ordinary dead cod. A lot of the small silver scales had flaked away but the single upward eye was still bulging and lifelike.

Margaret said quietly, "This part of the world is a natural refrigerator. This has been dead several days." She uncoiled the small lead on the black box and held the pseudo-microphone over the dead fish. Then she clicked a switch. Larren had guessed from the preparations what was about to happen, but still his mouth tightened as the geiger counter emitted its ominous crackle. The needle on the dial flickered as it registered a low degree of radio-activity.

After a moment she clicked the switch again and the crackle stopped. She laid the detector down and looked at Larren.

He said slowly, "Where did this come from?"

"From the cove that Cleyton was looking for when he went out into the blizzard. I went there with a party of Lapps as soon as the weather cleared, looking for his body. I couldn't find it, but when I got as far as the cove I did find the shoal of dead fish he was looking for, and out of curiosity I brought a couple back. I wondered what had killed them. I dissected one, and although I couldn't be sure I formed the impression that they had been killed by the shock of an explosion. I threw the dissected one away, and was going to throw this one after it, and then I accidentally happened to switch on the geiger counter and discovered that this one was radio-active."

"A shoal of dead fish killed by an explosion," Larren said thoughtfully. "And emitting radiation. That spells a nuclear explosion under the sea."

The doctor nodded. "That's what I thought."

"But it couldn't have been very large," Larren went on in the same tone. "Otherwise the vibrations would have been picked up in the U.S., the Americans are always on the alert for evidence of fresh Communist bomb tests. And if anything had been noticed it would have reached C.E. by normal intelligence channels." He swung towards the doctor with a sudden thought. "Why didn't you tell me this earlier?"

"Because you're not fit enough to do anything about it," she returned bluntly. "I would have told you tomorrow but it became obvious that you wouldn't rest until all your questions were answered."

Larren saw no cause to argue. He tried to think and finally said, "Did Cleyton know the fish were radio-active?"

"No. I didn't find the fish until after he'd vanished. One of the Lapps found the shoal originally and told me. I mentioned it to Cleyton, and I suppose he thought that it might possibly be important. He couldn't have guessed that they would turn out to be radio-active, but he could have realised that it was most probably an underwater explosion that had caused the whole shoal to be washed up."

Larren nodded. "That sounds plausible. With so many other odd things happening around here Cleyton would have undoubtedly decided to check it. I wonder if he ever reached that cove."

Margaret shrugged her shoulders. "I don't know. There was no sign. But if there had been the blizzard would have wiped it out. I only found the fish by digging for them in the snow. The man who found them had been pretty explicit about the spot."

As she talked she coiled up the lead

on the geiger counter again and returned the black box to its cupboard. Then she replaced the enamel bowl with the dead fish. Larren waited for her to finish and they returned in silence to her living quarters.

Larren sat down at the table again, for his head continued to torment him and his legs were decidedly unsteady. He picked up the whisky that he had left behind and drank it down. Then, while he still had the momentary flush of strength it gave him, he said:

"You said nothing about the fish when you radioed that Cleyton was missing — why?"

"Because I didn't want to sound a fool over the radio," she retorted coldly. "Not with half the hams in the world listening in. Besides, I didn't know until you turned up that Cleyton worked for counter-espionage. I had no reason to suspect foul play — or to think that the fish might be important."

Larren frowned and tried to think of anything that he might have missed. He set his glass down on the table and his hand caught it clumsily as he pulled away, rolling it over to topple off the edge of the table and land on one of the large rugs. The doctor stooped to pick up the fallen glass and replaced it on the table out of his reach. She said firmly:

"You can stop thinking up more questions because I'm not going to answer them. Not until you've had some sleep anyway. You must have some sense or you wouldn't have been picked for this job, so you must realise that you can't do a damned thing until you've given that head a chance to mend. You must rest."

Larren knew that with Joe Carver still unconscious it could prove fatal to let the doctor have her way. He still didn't know how much he could trust her, and at least one of them should remain awake all of the time now that he had revealed the true story of their faked crash. But at the same time he knew that Margaret Norstadt was right and that he was fit for nothing until his head wound had at least started to heal. Even now he could barely think straight, and concentration was an impossibility. Then he realised grimly that if Margaret Norstadt was against them and wanted them both unconscious then in his present condition she could quite easily achieve that aim by administering a sharp crack over his skull. Both he and Carver were committed to trusting her now, and there was not much that they could do about it. The clamouring pains in his head seemed to be bursting in one long and continuous explosion now and he knew that he had no choice but to capitulate.

He said reluctantly, "All right — I will rest."

She smiled. "You'll rest all right. Because I'm going to fix you a good sleeping draught that will keep you out for several hours. You need really deep sleep, and that's a doctor's order."

Something about both her tone and her smile sent a shiver of disquiet through Larren's mind, but his head was now aching so badly that he could not be sure that his senses had not got mixed up with his imagination. And then one last tangible thought emerged sharply from his sinking mental haze. Adrian Cleyton had been too good an agent to fall down on even a bad cover. How far had Cleyton trusted Margaret Norstadt?

6

No Choice but to Kill

The doctor's sleeping draught kept Larren out for just under twelve hours, but even then a further sixteen hours were to pass before he was able to take any action. By then his once-blinding headache had dwindled to an occasional stab that only affected him when he moved his head too quickly, and he decided that he was now fit enough to make his first move and visit the cove that had been Cleyton's last-known destination. He waited until the last hour before dawn, reasoning that he could get clear of Stadhaven in darkness and still be able to examine the cove in the brief hours of dwindling light that decreased daily as the continuous three-month night of Arctic mid-winter swiftly approached.

Margaret Norstadt objected strongly as he donned his furs, arguing that he was still too weak from his half-healed head wound to face up to the rigours of the Arctic night, but Larren waved her objections aside. He knew that from the medical viewpoint she was right, but time was now too scarce to justify any further delay. Carver's leg needed X-ray reports to make sure that it was setting properly and she had already radioed for a ship to come up and take them off. She had included details of Larren's fictitious injuries in her report as he had asked, and had the details on Carver tallied with those agreed upon before the two men had left Smith's office in Whitehall then Larren knew that the rescue ship would have been delayed to give them more time; as the report on Carver did not tally then Smith, who was in anonymous contact with the Norwegian authorities who received Margaret Norstadt's radio reports, would know that the stunt-pilot was genuinely hurt, and so the delaying tactics would not be employed. Larren couldn't afford to wait another twenty hours or more until the brief period of daylight came round again.

As he struggled into the last layer of clothing, the thickhooded fur parka, the blonde Norwegian doctor glared at him angrily and demanded:

"But what can you possibly hope to find out there? If any of the fish are left then they will be buried too deep in the snow for you to see anything. And if I couldn't find Cleyton's body with a search party of Lapp Eskimoes who know the island inside-out, upside-down and backwards how can you expect to do any better?"

Larren was busy adjusting his snow goggles that hung loose around his chin, for it hurt too much to push them above his eyes until needed, the strap pulled too tightly against his head wound. He paused and said grimly:

"I don't expect to do better. But I can find out whether any new shoals of radio-active fish have been washed up, or whether there are any fresh traces of under-sea explosions. And it will also give me an opportunity to study Barren Island across the straits." As he spoke he tapped the lumpy bulge of the powerful binoculars that hung in front of his chest beneath the parka.

Margaret continued to glare, more angry than ever as she realised that the last of her arguments had run out. She had changed her bright red-and-orange sweater for an equally bright yellow-and-green, and now she jerked down its rumpled waist-line with the determined gesture of a woman about to dress to go out.

"Then I'd better go with you," she declared flatly. "I let Cleyton wander off alone and he didn't come back — and he wasn't suffering from a crack across the head."

She moved towards her living quarters where her own furs hung behind the door and Larren's voice had an equally non-arguable tone as he stopped her.

"Don't bother. I'm going alone." She turned sharply, but before she could speak he rapped on, "You'll stay here to answer the questions of anyone who comes round. I don't want some curious islander to come looking for you because his little finger aches or his wife is having labour pains, and finding that you're not here and neither am I. Because once one of them finds out that I'm fit to prowl around then they'll all know. And I'm pretty sure that one of them must be receiving a frequent visitor from Barren; someone who exchanges a nice, shiny oil lamp or a ten-pound tin of whale fat just for the latest gossip."

Margaret hesitated. "You might get lost."

"I've got a compass. We're not quite far enough north for the magnetic pull of the pole to upset it."

"Didn't Cleyton have a compass?"

It was Larren's turn to hesitate, but only fractionally. "Cleyton wasn't expecting trouble. I'll be expecting anything."

There wasn't much more to be said, and it was Joe Carver who eventually broke the strained silence. The scar-faced pilot had recovered consciousness before Larren, but still lay helpless on his bed. Margaret had given him a morphia injection to cut down the pain and he was still awake. He had already apologised bitterly for becoming a liability and had cursed the *Death Drivers* crash that had first broken and weakened his leg. Since then he had done over two dozen crashes and similar stunt jobs for Smith and considered it sheer bad luck that the leg had given way again on this one. Now he said quietly:

"Larren's right, Doc. If you're not here to maintain our cover story then anyone can come wandering in to see who's here and who isn't. I can't move out of this damned bed to meet them in the doorway and insist that my friend is too sick to be disturbed. We're relying on you for that."

Carver's voice had exactly the right kind of persuasive tone, and was probably the only asset that the *Death Drivers* crash had left of his ability to charm a woman. Margaret Norstadt responded slightly, unappeased, but refraining from any further argument.

Larren slipped a large torch into the pocket of his parka, just in case he failed to get back before the short glimmer of daylight had passed, and then he lashed his fur-booted feet into light snow-shoes and drew on his gloves. Reluctantly Margaret Norstadt saw him outside.

Somewhere to his right was the Eskimo settlement of half-buried tents, but he could see nothing of it. He moved away fast and although he didn't think that anyone had seen him leave the medical post he couldn't be sure. His snow-shoes left a faint but clear trail, and he could only trust to luck and one of the frequent snow storms to cover his tracks before they were seen. It was another unavoidable gamble that he just had to take, and he was beginning to think that there were too many.

He stopped once and unzipped a barely-noticeable pocket below the knee of his thick fur trousers and lifted up the razoredged sheath knife fitted inside so that the hilt was free and could be grasped instantly. There was a Smith & Wesson .38 hidden in a similar, carefully-padded pocket in his parka, but a gun would be too awkward to handle with gloved hands. Besides, he preferred a knife in the dark, it was silent, and he was an expert, as he had told Margaret Norstadt, he was prepared for anything.

Mentally he reviewed what Smith had told him of her history as he crossed the island: Norwegian father and English mother; born in Norway; her mother died of T.B. when she was twelve; her father moved to Oslo and ultimately put her through university; she qualified as a doctor and became a medical officer for the Norwegian health authorities. Smith's voice seemed to quote on methodically in Larren's memory, reading extracts from a slim file like a bingo caller shouting numbers. Presumably she had had love affairs, but Smith knew of only one lengthy one shortly after she left university with another graduate named Olaf something. Smith had almost apologised for the blank spots there, but it was a hastily compiled file because no intelligence department had ever heard of her before his enquiries. There was absolutely nothing against her, except that she had volunteered to be stranded on an Arctic island to salvage a settlement of sick Eskimoes from marauding flu germs, and the fact that her arrival had coincided with a surge of mysterious Russian movement on the island next door. Was it merely coincidence?

Larren's mind tackled the problem from another angle and went back over the outbreak of the flu epidemic. Stadhaven was situated on a sheltered inlet that was used as a refuge and a rest post by the small Norwegian whaling boats that hunted farther north during the three-month period of complete daylight in midsummer, and it was assumed that some sick sailor had passed on the fever to the Lapp inhabitants. It was a whaling captain who had first alerted the Norwegian health authorities of the outbreak, and it was one of the larger whaling vessels that had provided Margaret Norstadt's transport and helped her to set up her temporary medical post. Now Larren began to ask himself whether the unproved theory that a Norwegian sailor had infected the Eskimoes might be wrong. Could the islanders have been deliberately exposed to infection from some other source merely to provide an opportunity for the Russians to plant an agent on Dog Island?

But that was absurd. And for what purpose? Larren had to remind himself that it was Margaret Norstadt's radioed reports that had alerted counter-espionage in the first place. She had reported the disappearance of the Eskimo, and the presence of the submarine in the straits, whereas if she was working for the Russians then surely her job would be to hush things up. To imagine that she had only reported the events to protect her cover was again absurd, for apart from the one boat that had been due to make a late-season call to take her off the island in five days' time, and was now approaching three days ahead of schedule on account of Carver and himself, nothing else would be touching Dog for the rest of the long Arctic winter.

Larren's brain went round in circles but came up with the same answer with every revolution: there was nothing solid against Margaret Norstadt. He had searched her living quarters thoroughly soon after he recovered consciousness after taking her sleeping draught, for she had left the medical post for a brief time to check on the last of her now fast-recovering patients. And he had found nothing that was not as it should be. He had conferred with Joe Carver, seeking the stunt-man's opinion, and Carver had been convinced that she was genuine. His concluding comment was that if she was acting a part then she was a far better actress than any in the movie business. But still Larren's doubts persisted. He didn't like coincidences, and someone must have put the finger on Cleyton. And there was something else — something obvious that he had missed. He had a worried feeling that he had failed to spot some glaring factor that would cause him to kick himself when it eventually clicked. He sensed vaguely that it stemmed from their first conversation, something that should have registered but for the fierce, blurring pain of the fresh wound in his head. It was that missing factor that was the main pivot of all his doubts.

The cold began to break up Larren's thoughts, penetrating gradually through the outer layers of his furs and gripping at his body, but even so they lasted him until he reached the cove. By this time the darkness had faded to a dim grey light over a white waste-land, and the short, four-hour day had begun. The wind still swept bitingly across the island, cutting in from a heaving dark-grey sea. Close to the shore the sea was frozen solid, but towards the mouth of the cove the ice had broken into a maze of large floes that crunched and grated together with the movement of the flattened waves. Barren Island was invisible through a haze of mist and cloud that filled the straits, and so too was the sun which Larren knew would be trickling like a half-submerged ball along the southern horizon.

He stared out across the straits for a moment, and then flapped his arms vigorously and pounded his gloved fists into the palms of his hands to re-vitalise his flagging circulation. Then he began a diligent search around the edge of the cove. He found nothing and moved out warily on to the ice, his movements becoming increasingly slower as he worked his way away from the shore on to the broken floes. He knew that to slip and fall into one of the cracked network of clear-water channels would spell his finish, for even if the weight of his furs did not drag him down below the surface he would freeze to death almost immediately on clawing his way back on to the ice. As he searched he wondered for the first time whether Cleyton's disappearance *could* have been an accident? Could the slim man have slipped amongst these very same ice floes? Or, if his body did rest beneath the ice-roofed sea under Larren's feet, had it been dumped there as the most effective way of covering up a murder?

Larren tried to force the thought from his mind and concentrated on the job in hand, but although he covered as much of the frozen cove as he dared he found no fresh shoals of dead fish. The glittering ice slabs were white and empty. He had taken off his snow-shoes in order to jump the spreading cracks of clear water, but as they became wider a clean, four-foot gap stopped him altogether. On any other terrain he could have taken it almost in his stride, but on the smooth ice where a slip would be fatal he allowed caution to prevail.

He turned his back to the sea and the wind and slipped one hand out of his outer glove just long enough to unfasten the throat of his parka and draw out the large binoculars. His fingers were slightly stiff with cold and clumsy inside two thin pairs of inner nylon gloves but he managed to fasten the parka again. He pulled his snow goggles down below his chin and then donned his glove again. The binoculars were still warm from contact with his body, but even so he flinched as he brought them to his eyes. Had he allowed them to dangle outside his parka in the bitter air the icy metal would have frozen to his skin, unremovable without tripping off the outer layer with which the rims had made contact. He turned slowly to face the sea again, and stared out in the direction of Barren Island.

He saw nothing. He was using the most powerful binoculars that money could buy; but even they could not penetrate the thick bank of grey mist that blotted out the Soviet land-mass across the straits.

He didn't swear, for it was hopeless to expect anything in this visibility, he simply stared sourly for a moment and then dropped the range of the binoculars to sweep over the ice floes beyond the deep gap at his feet. He moved the glasses with painstaking slowness and spent fifteen minutes in carefully probing the sea-washed floes beyond his reach. Again there was nothing to see. Not a single fish, radio-active or otherwise, marred the scratches and crevices across the glassy, frozen slabs that the powerful lenses sucked close to his eyes.

Finally the cold that gnawed into him as he stood immobile forced him to give up the search. He raised the binoculars momentarily in the direction of the hidden island across the mist-draped sea and then turned away.

He dropped the binoculars and spent another vigorous five minutes in trying to beat some warmth back into his shivering body.

Once his blood began to circulate again he picked his way tentatively back to the reassuring solidity of the shore. He knew now that there was nothing to be found here at the cove, and as long as the combination of cloud and mist existed there was no hope of examining Barren from a distance. His trek out here had told him nothing and now he must plan another move.

He reached his snow-shoes and strapped them on again, and then replaced his goggles to protect his eyes from the biting wind. He fumbled to insert the binoculars back beneath his parka just in case the mist should clear and give him an opportunity to use them properly, but after an hour and a half of stamping around and flailing his arms in uncomfortable waiting he knew it was pointless to delay any longer. The greyness was darkening and the invisible sun that had never fully surfaced must be now sinking down below the southern horizon. He turned his back on the wind and the grinding of the harsh sea and ice-scape behind him and began the cold trudge back to Stadhaven.

He moved swiftly across the snow, spurred by the sting of the elements. Night began to blot out the inhospitable white world and the wind blew harder. Larren's mind began to back-track over the thoughts that had occupied him on his way out and he reviewed again the problem of Margaret Norstadt. For half an hour as he plodded homewards the endless circles revolved round in his brain. And then quite suddenly the missing factor clicked into place.

The geiger counter!

What did a bona fide doctor want with a geiger counter?

Larren stopped in mid-stride. It was the obvious question that he should have asked when she had demonstrated the radiation content in the dead fish, but his head had been too full of pain. For a moment he was motionless, thinking hard, and then equally abruptly the new implications lost importance.

There was a quick lunge of movement as a fur-padded shape straightened up from behind a hummock of ice less than three paces away, and Larren saw the quickly levelled angle of the crude Lapp hunting spear as it swung up towards his chest. The spear thrust with the man's full weight behind it, and instinctively Larren guessed that this was exactly how it had happened to Cleyton.

But Larren had been subconsciously prepared ever since he had left Stadhaven for something of this kind. Now he swayed, leaning sideways to grasp the hilt of the knife that protruded above the low pocket of his trouser leg as the bone-tipped spear-point snagged in the fur of his parka beneath his left arm. His gloved left hand closed swiftly on the haft of the spear and he hurled himself backwards as the knife came free in his right. The strength of his pull and his attacker's own momentum jerked the man off balance and he stumbled forwards. As he fell down on top of

Larren so the Britisher's knife swept up, and the force of the impact drove the keen six-inch blade deeply home.

Larren rolled as the corpse landed on top of him, turning them both over and rising swiftly to one knee astride the body. He drew the knife smoothly free in the same moment and tensed for any fresh attack.

None came. His would-be murderer had been alone.

For a few moments Larren remained crouching, listening to the wind howling across the black Arctic landscape. Then he turned his attention to the man he had killed. The body was short and squat, and the face inside the deep hood was the wrinkled yellow-brown face of a Lapp Eskimo. The man looked to be in his forties, his eyes were tightly closed but his mouth gaped open slightly, still retaining an unuttered exclamation of agony.

Carefully Larren wiped his knife-blade on the dead man's furs, and then he slipped the blade back into the special sheath next to his right calf. He wondered thoughtfully who had paid the Eskimo to try and kill him, and his thought process ended logically with the fact that only Margaret Norstadt had known where he was going.

7

A Distasteful Half-Hour

It was an hour later before Larren saw the long wooden outline of the hospital hut emerging from the windswept gloom ahead, and despite the fact that the bitter cold had now soaked into every bone he slowed his pace cautiously. He reached the outer door without receiving any sign to alarm him and quietly pushed it open. He stepped swiftly into the corridor inside, closed the door equally silently behind him and hoped that the sudden inrush of night wind had not caused any noticeable draught beneath any of the doors leading off the corridor.

He listened for a moment, satisfied himself that no one seemed aware of his return, and then knelt to remove his snow-shoes. He brushed the snow that had fallen in the last hour from his shoulders and then removed his gloves.

He rubbed his hands hard together to ease out the stiffness and then divested himself of his outer furs. It was still cold here in the empty corridor and he shivered a little as he unzipped the padded pocket in his parka and transferred the Smith and Wesson .38 to his jacket. Then he quietly pushed open the door of the hospital ward and went inside.

He was almost surprised to find Joe Carver still lying comfortably in his bed. Carver's scarred face relaxed and the automatic in his hand that had been covering the doorway lowered apologetically.

Carver said calmly, "Don't be so quiet the next time you approach. You could get — "

Larren shook his head in a slight gesture of warning and said softly, "Where's Doctor Margaret?"

Carver stared at him, and then the cold expression in Larren's grey-green eyes gave him a hint of what had happened. He said equally softly, "She's in there." And gestured to the door that led to the doctor's living quarters. Then he added,

"What went wrong?"

Larren moved closer to the ever-burning oil stove in the centre of the room and thawed the last frozen wrinkles out of his hands. The blood tingled in his fingers and then he answered Carver's question.

"Somebody tried to spear me."

Carver watched in uneasy silence as he crossed the small hospital ward and opened the door to Margaret Norstadt's living quarters. The room was hot from the glowing stove in the centre and the oil lamp was burning. The doctor wasn't there but the door to her bedroom stood slightly open. Larren gently closed the door behind him. For a moment he hesitated in the empty room, and then he drew out the Smith and Wesson from his jacket pocket. He circled around the room and the oil lamp on the table threw his shadow in huge, menacing movement around the wall.

Larren stepped inside the bedroom. There was a third oil stove burning against the wall and beside it was a low camp bed. Margaret Norstadt lay lazily on the bed, beneath the blankets but still wearing her roll-necked yellow-and-green sweater. She was propped on one elbow and reading a novel. She glanced up as he entered.

"Larren, don't you knock when — " And then she saw the efficient little gun in his hand.

Larren said quietly, "Get up, Doctor."

Anger registered sharply in her eyes, but not fear. She stared not at the gun but straight at his face.

"What is this — rape?"

He shook his head. "You know better than that. The man you sent to kill me made a mess of it. You should have told him that I was more prepared than Cleyton."

"You're talking nonsense. That crack on the head must have caused more damage than I — "

"*Get up*, Doctor." Larren's tone was not loud but the emphasis on the first two words were chilling in effect.

Slowly Margaret Norstadt pushed back her blankets and stood up. Although she still wore her sweater she had removed her slacks and her legs were bare, long smooth legs that would delight a connoisseur. Larren tried not to look at her legs, or to notice the fact that the lower edge of the woollen sweater only descended as far as her hips and that despite the Arctic surroundings her underwear was as distractingly black and feminine as that of any London fashion model.

He said bluntly, "Why was Cleyton killed? Did he find out anything, or was he just a nuisance?"

"Cleyton got lost in a blizzard, you know — "

Larren stepped a pace closer. "I could make you strip off that sweater as well," he warned. "Three minutes outside in your panties and bra and you'll be glad to talk. It's at least twenty below zero out there."

The first flicker of fear showed through, and she glanced down at herself, acknowledging for the first time that she was only half-dressed.

"You wouldn't dare."

Larren said harshly, "Adrian Cleyton was a good friend of mine, he pulled me out of a couple of hot spots in Greece. Now he's dead. And an hour ago one of your precious Lapp Eskimoes tried to impale me with his spear." His free hand shot out suddenly and grabbed the bottom edge of the sweater. She flinched and made a frantic effort to twist away but his hand knotted in the heavy wool, tightening it around her waist and pulling her closer. He finished flatly, "Right now there's not much that I wouldn't dare do."

She swallowed hard and he could feel the uncontrolled panic rising in her straining body.

"If one of the Lapps did attack you I still don't know anything about it. And if I had had a hand in killing Cleyton do you think that I would have reported the fact that he was missing to my superiors."

Larren rested the weight of the Smith and Wesson almost casually between her breasts, the snub nose pressing against her. "Of course you would," he said grimly. "Because it would have looked too bad for you if you had failed to report him missing after he had stopped making contact with London."

"I tell you I know nothing about it," she argued desperately.

"I think you know too much about it. How long have you been working for the Reds?"

"Oh God," she said helplessly. "I'm just a doctor, that's all. I don't know anything about the Reds. I don't know anything about your business. And I don't want to know anything."

Larren twisted her sweater into an even tighter knot that bored his fist hard into her stomach. He felt her quiver of revulsion and jabbed with the point of his automatic just for good measure.

"Suppose you tell me what an ordinary doctor needs with a geiger counter," he demanded.

The question had no effect except to make her blink. "The geiger counter," she repeated blankly. And then she almost laughed, her expression becoming faintly hysterical. "Surely you're not suspicious because of that!"

"Tell me anyway."

She recovered herself. "The geiger counter belongs to a friend of mine. He studied geology at university while I was studying medicine. Since then I've spent a couple of working holidays with him. I took an interest in his work because I'm interested in him. When he heard that I was coming up here to Dog he asked me to look out for any unusual rock samples if I had the time. He loaned me the counter and I promised to switch it on at various spots on the island and let him know the results."

"You take a lot of interest in your friends' hobbies."

"With this friend yes." She was suddenly resentful of his prying. "I might marry him one day."

Larren issued one of his rare smiles. "The story is too pat. Tell me why you really brought that geiger counter up here? What did you expect to find? What were you *told* to look for?"

"I wasn't told to look for anything. I've told you the truth." Her voice was becoming desperate once more. "If I did have any — any secret reasons for bringing a geiger counter up here do you think I would have been fool enough to drag it out in front of you only five minutes after you had told me that you were a British agent?"

That thought had not escaped Larren on the last part of his journey back from the cove, and had added to his confusion, but now he simply brushed it aside.

"It's an old trick to draw attention to yourself, hoping to avoid suspicion by appearing too obvious. And I'm too old to fall for it."

"Oh God," she said again. "What can I say to convince you?"

"Nothing," Larren said flatly. "The man I had to kill tonight followed me out to that cove. And only you knew that I was going there. Only you could have sent him."

He stared hard into her eyes, seeing real fear in their silver-grey depths, and then he steeled himself for what he had to do next. He dropped his automatic back into his pocket and said calmly:

"I'm sorry about this, doctor. But you're playing in a big-time league where nobody can afford to take chances. But you know that don't you? That's why you sent your spear-man after Cleyton and then me. And that's why I can't take the risk of letting you live."

As he spoke he released her sweater and clamped both hands swiftly around her throat.

Margaret Norstadt fought frantically as his hands closed, but his feet were braced and his body rock-steady. She clawed at the backs of his hands, trying to drag his fingers away, her body writhing and crushed sounds gargling deep in her throat as she tried to scream. Her eyes bulged and slowly and inexorably he strangled her.

Her struggles became weaker until her body was a dead weight in his hands. Only then did he release her throat and catch her by the shoulders to lower her to the floor. He was now as sure as he could possibly be that Doctor Margaret was not a Russian agent and swiftly turned her face down and extended her arms above her head. He knelt astride her hips and pressed his hands around her waist, pushing up beneath the ribs. He applied artificial respiration for several minutes until he was sure that her laboured breathing was back to normal regularity. Then he straightened up and lifted her gently on to the camp bed.

For a moment he looked down at her, feeling slightly sick and foully tainted by the whole dirty business of espionage and counter-espionage, and then he covered up the limp, bare legs with the blankets and turned away.

He went back into the living-room, found the whisky bottle and poured himself a stiff drink. He didn't think that he had ever spent a more distasteful half-hour in his life, but he could think of no other way in which it could be done.

After a moment he found a second glass, and returned with both glasses and the bottle to the doctor's bedroom. He drew a chair up beside her bed and then drank down another stiff whisky. It did nothing for his conscience and his head began to ache. The bluish bruise marks on Margaret's throat were very prominent and he couldn't help looking at them as he started on the task of bringing her round.

It took him ten minutes of gently massaging her cheeks and moistening her throat and temples with a damp handkerchief, and when her eyes finally opened he was supporting her head and shoulders with one arm. Her body shuddered beneath the blankets and he winced at the surge of terror that rushed into her eyes. He smiled as gently as he knew how and said softly:

"Try and sip this, Doctor. You came through with flying colours."

She remained still as he pressed the glass to her lips, her body still tense and her eyes uncertain.

Larren said, "I'm sorry I had to do that. But I had to know for certain whether you were working against me or not. I was pretty sure of you after all the questions, but I had to be one hundred per cent sure. That's why I had to get rough. That strangle-hold was a pretty basic one, and anyone with any kind of spy-training could have broken it easily in two or three different ways. But you didn't. You haven't had any spy-training and you don't know the counter moves. You're not a trained agent, and if you were a dabbling amateur it would have showed up under my questioning. I'm very sorry."

She tried to speak, coughed, and then said weakly:

"Did you have to damn-nigh kill me?"

He nodded. "I did. A good agent could have held out until the last moment in the hope that I was bluffing. If you were a good agent you would have waited until the last moment before blacking out before attempting to break my hold. And with my own and Carver's lives possibly resting on it I had to be absolutely sure of you."

She pushed his hand away, still without tasting the whisky in the offered glass. She said bitterly:

"You're a regular Nazi, aren't you."

Larren said nothing as she sat upright on the camp bed. She touched her throat gingerly and then turned to look at him, the returning anger building up in her eyes.

"Now that you've proved your point you can get out of my bedroom. And stay out."

"Not just yet," Larren's voice was quiet. "I need your help."

She stared at him. "You need my help!" There was amazement in her voice and her anger was rising rapidly to fury. "I'd as soon kiss Himmler or Eichmann as help a swine like you. If you were alone I'd quite happily yell the truth about you into the radio until your blasted Russians come to collect you. But I won't for the sake of that poor devil out there with the broken leg. But I'll see you deep in hell before I'll actually help you."

Larren waited for her outburst to subside and then said flatly, "You'll help me. I simply want you to speak to the Lapps and translate a request before they have time to miss the man that I had to kill. I want a boat, a kayak if nothing else is available, to take me across to Barren Island. It's the only way left to find out what is really going on over there."

She glared at him. "Ask them yourself."

Larren's mouth tightened and he realised that he had no choice but to get rough with her again. He said harshly:

"Don't be foolish, Doctor. You can't simply stand to one side and ignore what's happening around you. Cleyton is gone and I only just survived a murder attempt tonight. If another attempt is made to eliminate me it will probably include Carver — and it will include you too because it will be assumed that you know too much. You're on our side whether you like it or not."

8

Through Frozen Seas

It took Larren another ten minutes to convince Margaret Norstadt that unless she intended to defect fully to the other side then she really did have no choice but to help him. The fact that she had maintained his cover story of an accidental crash by radioing the details of his supposed injuries would leave the enemy in no doubt that he and Carver had been forced to take her at least partly into their confidence. When she finally faced the inescapable fact that she could not stand aside or in the middle she became even more bitter. She was intelligent enough to realise that he was right and that if the Russians did decide to liquidate Larren and Carver then they would have to silence her also. She capitulated at last and agreed to help him find a boat, as she spoke she accepted the glass of whisky that he offered her the second time and glowered at him with hate in her eyes.

Larren stood up and said quietly, "You'd better get dressed as soon as you feel fit to go out, because I want that boat straight away. The wind's not too strong at the moment and the seas are about as passable as I can hope for this late in the year, and I want to make the crossing over to Barren while I've got the chance. If I wait for daylight to come round again the odds are that it might be blowing a blizzard."

Margaret said nothing, and after a few moments he turned away. He knew that he could rely on her co-operation, and he knew that he could quite safely leave the crippled Carver in her care. He had satisfied himself that she was nothing more than the volunteer doctor that she appeared to be. But when he saw the loathing in her eyes he wondered whether it was worth the price. He left her to get dressed and closed the bedroom door behind him. There was a foul taste in his mouth, and at the moment he was the foulest thing around.

He went back into the small hospital ward and found Joe Carver alert and awaiting his return. The stunt-pilot was still lying relaxed, but his eyes were wary and Larren guessed that the hand hidden beneath the bedclothes still retained the automatic.

Carver said, "I heard raised voices once or twice. What happened?"

Larren told him, briefly but fully. Carver's scarred face tightened when he related the fact that he had throttled Margaret Norstadt completely unconscious before being fully satisfied.

"Was that really necessary?"

Larren had not expected Carver to approve, but Carver was a specialist, recruited for his own particular skill and not an experienced field operator. Larren explained his reasons but Carver's expression did not change. He realised then that it was just as well that he hadn't given the doctor a chance to scream or he would have wound up fighting his own ally.

Carver said at last, "So now you're

satisfied." He was trying to keep the contempt out of his voice and accept the fact that he could do nothing about an incident that was over. He was silent for a moment and then went on, "But if she didn't send the Eskimo after you, have you started wondering who did?"

Larren nodded. "I've thought about it, and now I think that in this case no one did actually send him. I think that someone paid him to eliminate Cleyton, and that when he saw me heading for the same taboo area of the cove he quite happily thought that he could earn another packet of salt, or whatever they paid him, by spearing me too. Perhaps he was asked to keep an eye on you and I after the plane crashed. If I had the time I'd get Doctor Margaret to help me question the rest of the Lapps to try and verify that the dead man was receiving visitors from Barren. But I must get over to that other island now while the weather is relatively calm and before the islanders find that body and refuse me a boat for killing one of their fellows. Besides, the answers to the mystery must all lie on

Barren Island — and the Eskimoes here can't tell us anything that will really help to clear it up."

Carver had no comment to make and after a moment Margaret Norstadt came into the room. She was now fully dressed and had pulled on an extra-thick woollen sweater. Her face was still just a little pale in its frame of yellow-blonde hair, but her expression was blank.

"I'm ready," she stated flatly.

Larren hesitated. She still looked shaken.

"It's not exactly life or death stuff yet," he said. "Wait another ten minutes."

She ignored him and turned away behind the door of her living quarters, and he heard the rustle of her outer furs as she removed them from the hook. He was aware of Carver's unfriendly gaze on his back as he watched her return to view with the furs in her arms. His unsmiling mouth compressed a little harder and he turned towards the corridor door to don his own furs.

He dressed quickly and returned the Smith and Wesson to its concealed pocket in his outer parka. The sheath knife in his trouser leg he again adjusted so that the handle was clear and easily reached. He had no illusions about his position now, and for all practical purposes he was alone. Joe Carver was helpless with his broken leg, and the doctor would only help as much as she had to, and that unwillingly. Strangely enough, Larren's face relaxed at the thought, for he preferred to work alone. The only snag was that he would still be responsible for Carver and the doctor if things went wrong.

He went back into the hospital ward and found Margaret zipping up her parka. She began to smoothe the first pair of nylon inner gloves over her hands and he waited until she had finished before speaking.

"Is it possible to borrow a kayak without the Eskimoes knowing? With luck they might think that it was washed away and not realise that I've taken it to cross over to Barren."

She hesitated and then looked up at his face. For a moment she still remained silent, fighting with her conscience, and then she said bitterly:

"I've got a small motor boat. You can borrow that. Most of the Eskimoes' tents are strung out along the inlet and the boat was the quickest way of visiting my patients during the summer before the water froze over." She stopped a moment and then went on, "I was tempted to let you go your own way and steal a kayak. The seas are almost certain to roll it over before you can get as far Barren, and although I don't doubt that you could roll it upright again you would have frozen in wet furs. But that would have been a kind of murder. There's a good chance that the seas will overturn my boat too, but at least there'll be nothing on my conscience if I give you the best boat available."

Larren thanked her. In the circumstances there was not much else that he could say, and he was not prepared to continue apologising. He waited while she pulled on a second pair of nylon gloves, followed by heavy fur mittens, and then she was ready. He allowed her to lead the way outside.

130

It took her ten minutes to find the boat. It was housed in a small hut on the bank of the inlet that was almost buried beneath a piled-up drift of snow. The door was not locked but Larren had difficulty in dragging it open against the weight of the hampering snow. Inside, the boat was well-buried beneath sacks and a tarpaulin. They both pushed inside, ducking their heads to miss the low roof, and stared at the blanketed shape.

Margaret said doubtfully, "I don't know if it will start. I haven't been able to use it since the inlet froze over."

Larren didn't answer but set to work to uncover the boat. The tarpaulin was frozen stiff like a sheet of crumpled concrete and it took him all his strength to crack it and push it away. The sacks beneath were also frozen but gave him less trouble. When it was revealed the craft proved to be a broad-beamed twelve-footer, painted a smart grey-blue and fitted with a low, sporty windshield. Larren eyed it dubiously. For a calm day's cruise on the Norfolk Broads it would have been ideal, but for six miles of open Arctic seas it didn't look so good.

"I think we can start it," he said. "The engine doesn't seem to be damaged. You kept it well protected." He moved around the cramped hut, the discarded sacks crackling under his feet. She stepped out of the way as he gave the bows a push and the small craft moved backwards with a slight grating sound. He pushed harder and once the stern started to slide on to the ice of the inlet it moved easily out of the hut.

"How far is the inlet frozen?" he asked.

"About two hundred yards, then it's cracked ice floes the rest of the way."

"It shouldn't be difficult." Larren began to push the light craft along the ice, and after a few moments she moved ahead and bent over the boat to help him.

They reached the edge of the unbroken ice and Larren used his torch as he probed around for a suitably wide channel. After a moment he found one and with the doctor's help he launched the boat into the icey seas. She knelt on the ice and steadied the boat as he took off his snow-shoes and climbed aboard.

It took him twenty minutes to get a spark from the cold engine, and another ten to get it really started. The exertion kept him warm but by then Margaret was shivering with cold as she crouched on the ice, the snow was still falling and her shoulders and the hood of her parka were thick with settled flakes. Once the engine was running Larren said quietly:

"Thanks, Doctor. You've done all you can. Now get back to the hut and relax."

She hesitated before letting go of the boat.

"There's a small bottle of brandy in that cubbyhole by the wheel," she said at last. "You may need it by the time you get across."

Larren looked at her, slightly surprised, but her face was pinched with cold and he could not read her expression. He nodded slowly and then settled into his place at the wheel. He opened the throttle and she pushed the boat clear of the ice to start him on his way.

She straightened up, shivering uncontrollably as he vanished into the night without looking back. Her emotions were hopelessly confused. She bitterly resented the tall Britisher's ruthless methods of ascertaining where her loyalties lay and she was still badly shaken from his rough handling. Yet at the same time she was glad that he was on her side. A short while ago she had been almost prepared to let him risk his life in a frail kayak, but now she felt horribly alone and unprotected without him.

She finally turned and hurried at a stumbling run back to the medical post.

Larren completely forgot the blonde Norwegian doctor within two minutes of leaving her behind, for the broken ice floes made steering and navigation two full-time jobs that wholly occupied his mind. The sea became rougher as he reached the mouth of the inlet, slapping into the little boat and pitching her bows up over the crests of the waves. A jagged white barrier of ice caused him to spin the wheel violently to avoid it, and when it was past his heartbeat was only slightly slower than a burst of tracer fire.

The boat began sliding into the troughs of eight feet waves and he realised thankfully that he had reached the open sea. The frail craft was riding the waves well and only shipping the sheets of spray that skimmed off the rearing crests. Larren crouched low behind the flimsy protection of the windshield and steeled himself for a grim trip.

He was aware of the grave possibility of being swept down through the straits and out into the black wastes of the Arctic Ocean, but at the moment the wind was coming directly across the straits and unless the direction veered either right or left he felt that it was unlikely that he could miss Barren. The island had a ten-mile coastline and was only six miles away, and he knew from the charts he had studied before leaving London that there were no detrimental currents.

After half an hour he was frozen stiff. His arms and wrists ached from holding the wheel and flying spray had coated the hood and shoulders of his parka with ice. More ice had frozen across the windshield and over the glass of his snow goggles. He was blind and shivering and his teeth chattered hard enough to break.

If there had been any choice he would have turned round and headed back, for he knew then that this trip was madness. But the seas had climbed higher and to try and bring the small boat round would almost certainly result in the waves turning her over. He had to keep her bows into the oncoming seas.

The snow was falling heavily and being ripped into flying streamers by the teeth of the wind. The seas loomed like charging humpbacks out of the black hell of the night. The boat nose-dived down countless valleys of rushing water and reared desperately through countless climbs with her bows pouring spray. Larren had no way of knowing whether he was making any progress or not, and wished that death was warmer.

Somehow he stayed conscious, despite the savage cold. Somehow he retained enough life in his wrists and arms to continue fighting the wheel. The agonising numbness had gripped every bone and even if he reached land he doubted whether he could ever move his frozen body from its cramped sitting position in the low cockpit. Another half-hour passed, and then another, and he began to wonder why he was fighting. He had underrated the Arctic and it was going to cost him his life. It would be so much easier just to let go of the wheel, and then let the oncoming seas swing the bows round and bury him.

He was tempted, but his gloved hands had locked on the wheel and would not let go. And then abruptly a ridge of ice loomed up at him out of the rushing darkness, it seemed to hover over him, swung to one side, and then was blotted out behind a squall of snow and spray. He heard the grinding of two large floes jostling together and in the same moment the wind and waves began to lose their force and he realised that he was in more sheltered seas and almost on top of Barren.

Somehow he moved his stiff finger to shut down the throttle and then he was moving slowly into calmer waters between drifting floes. He saw the edge of the main ice sheet ahead and pulled desperately to avoid smacking into it, and then followed the ice's edge. He found a gap and followed the channel inland, and simply kept going until the boat crunched and jammed itself between the two sides.

The engine stalled, and for a few moments he lacked the will to move. Then he made an effort to stir his frozen legs and winced as the hot pains shot through them. The fear that the boat might be holed and still sink beneath him gave him the will to slump sideways with his head and chest across the flat ice, and after a few moments his groping fingers found a crack. He made another effort and dragged his numb limbs slowly out of the jammed motor boat and on to the ice. His body sagged face downwards and he collapsed. The snow began to drift down on to his ice-coated shoulders and the wind sang its banshee wail into the black night.

9

Sniper in the Snow

For perhaps half a minute Larren lay
face down on the ice, and then slowly
his dominant brain took over. He had
crossed the straits and reached his goal
of Barren Island, and now that he had
escaped the icy tomb of the sea it was
too ironic to simply lay down and die.
He had to move.

He twisted round painfully in the
snow, crawling back to the edge of the
ice and flopping down full length again
as he reached into the boat he had just
left. He remembered Margaret Norstadt's
parting words and fumbled with frozen
fingers to drag open the closed panel
concealing the little cubbyhole beside the
wheel. His fingers scratched clumsily at
the catch and then his glove snagged and
pulled the panel down. He could see
the flat half-flask lying in the opening,

but he couldn't grip it with one hand, his fingers were extended stiffly and he couldn't make them close.

Almost sobbing he dragged himself a little farther over the edge of the ice, risking a fall back into the boat or into the freezing water of the channel. He got both hands into the opening, pressing the flask between them and dragging it out. Then he twisted away from the ice's edge, gripping the flask desperately like a performing seal using its flippers as he rolled over on to his back.

He pulled down his face mask, now stiff with frozen spray, and struggled clumsily to his knees. His teeth were still chattering insanely but he managed to bite the cap on the flask and twist. After taking a couple of fresh bites he spat the cap on the ice and tipped the life-giving brandy to his mouth.

A good measure spilled down his chin, for his hands were still shaking from the cold, but some of the raw spirit burned down into his stomach. He gasped and choked, and then swallowed another gulping mouthful. Tears stung his eyes and he decided that nothing had ever tasted better.

He took another long pull and felt life stirring through his heat-starved limbs, but he knew that he had drunk enough and that now he must move to remain alive. He set the flask down on the ice as carefully as he could with shivering hands, and then moved away from it for fear of knocking it over. The brandy had given him new heart and he began to beat his hands together in an effort to restore the circulation of his blood.

He realised later that he had been lucky, for a few yards away a large ice floe had been pushed up on to one side by its fellows and had remained in that position when the main ice sheet froze over, and it was this natural wind-break that sheltered him where he had landed. The snow was still falling, but the snow was nothing compared to the blessing of this brief escape from the raw bite of the below-zero wind. Without it he doubted whether he could have survived.

He beat his arms across his chest until they ached and then turned his attention to his legs. After being jammed unable to move in the small boat for an hour and a half they were completely paralysed with cold. He couldn't massage any warmth back into them but he did the next best thing and hammered them mercilessly with his fists until the feeling began to return. The next few minutes were some of the most agonising of his life as the blood began to flow again, surging like a sea of red-hot needle-points from hips to toes. As the pain increased he continued to hammer with his fists in a demoniac fury of self-punishment.

At last he stopped. He was still shivering and his teeth still chattered, but there was feeling in his body and he was unquestionably alive.

He made an attempt to stand up then, and his weak, shaking legs immediately collapsed beneath him. He made another try and this time balanced upright and took one step before falling. He told himself grimly that he was damned if he was still going to die after all this and pushed himself off the ice for the third time. This time he made three faltering steps before he fell and he was convinced that ultimately he could do it.

He spent the next five minutes in stumbling and falling about the ice, gradually staying on his feet a few seconds longer with each attempt. He moved in blind circles and the first time that he strayed from the protection of his wind-break the gale-force blast knocked him straight over. For a moment he tasted defeat, but Simon Larren had been too close to death too many times to even consider giving up. His determination came back and he crawled behind the shelter of the up-ended ice wall and struggled upright once more. He did a few more practice circles and then faced the wind again. He swayed on trembling legs and numbed feet, but he could stand.

He fumbled in the pocket of his parka for a torch and then played its beam across the ice as he searched for his precious brandy flask. He found it easily because the sheltering ice floe had prevented him from wandering too far away. He drank another warming mouthful and then searched for the cap. He found it, and although his fingers were still too unsteady to replace it he managed to get it back between his teeth and screwed the flask on to it. He thrust the flask into his pocket and then retrieved his snow-shoes from the boat. He sat down behind the merciful windbreak and clumsily but patiently affixed the snow-shoes to his feet.

It took an effort of will to come out from the lee of the ice floe and head inland across the frozen fringe of the sea, but Larren made it after only the briefest hesitation. The howling wind lashed him across the face and brought fresh tears to his eyes, for his useless, ice-encrusted goggles hung slackly beneath his chin. He bowed his head low and used one shielding hand to protect his eyes while the other directed the torch at his feet to guard against any sudden channels in the ice. He left Margaret Norstadt's small grey-blue boat behind without making any effort to mark its position, for he knew now that he could never hope to make the return crossing in his present state. The craft was too small and it would be madness to risk his life in it again now that he had experienced the full savagery of the Arctic seas. If he was fated to return to Dog then he would have to find some larger form of transport.

He moved away from the sea to eliminate the danger of plunging through any cracks in the ice, and then turned north. He carried a mental picture of the map of Barren that he had studied in Smith's office and he knew that the new structures that had attracted the attention of the Norwegian fisheries plane were situated at the northern end. Theoretically he had only to follow the coastline until he found them, for the map showed no bays or inlets to bar his path. He kept the sound of the ice floes just within hearing on his left to prevent himself from straying too far inland.

He tried to work out his position as he walked but it was purely guesswork. He thought that the wind had shifted round fractionally during the last half-hour of crossing the straits and that he should have landed somewhere north of the centre of Barren's ten-mile coastline. But how far north was impossible to judge. He just had to keep walking.

He tried not to dwell upon the consequences of missing the vaguely-described landing stage and other buildings he had been sent to find, for they offered his only hope of escape from Barren Island. Margaret Norstadt had talked of hearing boat engines in the night, and in obtaining one of these mystery boats, something bigger than the cockleshell in which he had arrived, lay his only hope of survival. The completion of his assignment was of secondary importance now, for the answers to the mystery surrounding Barren would be of no help to either him or Smith unless he was capable of returning to Dog.

His legs became increasingly heavy, and his feet solidly numb. The cold began to creep back into his body again and he stopped frequently to flap his arms and rub at his legs. He was tiring and he knew that if he allowed the cold to really grip him a second time then exhaustion would drag him down and there would be no hope of a second revival.

Then, after two hours of forced movement, the ice field finished and he stumbled to a halt at the very edge with his torch shining down on to a gleam of lapping black water.

There was no sign of the ice continuing across the evil glimmer of water, and perhaps three seconds passed before he realised that this deep channel slashing in from the sea must be man-made. Obviously there was no point in building a landing stage without maintaining a clear passage to the open sea. As the thought registered he automatically switched off his torch and stood motionless in the bitter, moonless night.

There was nothing to be seen, and nothing to be heard. He pushed back the hood of his parka for a moment, wincing as the raw wind stung his ears, but again there was nothing except an increase in the constant sounds of ice grinding somewhere out towards the sea and the whine of the wind. He hurriedly pulled the thick fur hood back into place.

He started to turn inland, where he was now sure he would find the assumed landing stage that the unknown Norwegian pilot had spotted from the air, and then an alien sound reached him from the opposite direction, towards the mouth of the open channel. It was almost the sound of ice upon ice as he had been hearing all the way along the coast, but not quite. He turned and followed the channel towards the open sea, staring hard into the darkness across the ugly black water. He stopped again as the first suggestion of angular line became vaguely visible in the gloom.

He knew then that he had definitely not heard ice upon ice, but the scratching of ice upon steel. There was a large patrol boat of some kind lying without lights in the mouth of the cut, and a drifting floe must have touched her hull as it passed. He could only distinguish the angle of the bows, but their slant and height indicated a motor torpedo boat or something similar in size. He remembered standing only a few yards away with his torch flashing and wondered whether it was possible that he had not been seen. Anyone standing on the mystery vessel's deck must have seen him.

However, the ship continued to lie in silence and darkness, and after a few moments he turned away, moving cautiously inland along the edge of the channel. He had to watch his step on the smooth ice, but more than anything his senses were fully alert for the first long-expected sign that he was not alone in the Arctic night.

After three minutes he saw the landing stage, constructed solidly of concrete at the inland end of the cut. He was almost on top of it before he saw that it was grey and not a continuation of the glassy white ice, and that although flat surfaced it was roughened and not slippery smooth, and even then it was only the sight of the large motor launch tied up against it that really convinced him. There was still no sign of any welcoming committee and he moved closer.

The landing stage was simply a

concrete wall at the end of the inlet, but it was almost thirty feet across and several feet higher than the bulwarks of the launch. Obviously it had been constructed to serve bigger craft, but what had been landed here to necessitate such a stalwart structure?

Larren walked out on to the blanket of frozen snow that covered the concrete and glanced down over the edge. The launch was completely unattended and looked like a gift from heaven — until he wondered how he could possibly take it out past the larger patrol boat in the channel mouth.

He decided to forget about the launch for a few moments at least and moved away from the quay's edge to explore farther afield. Visibility was still thirty or forty yards but he could see nothing that could explain the presence of the landing stage, and nothing of whatever had been landed. The grey-white terrain, moving into darkness, was completely flat.

The complete absence of any kind of guards puzzled him, and he could only suppose that whoever had built the landing stage and owned the launch must consider themselves absolutely safe from stray intruders. Then he remembered how close he had brushed with death in getting here and decided that perhaps their attitude was understandable. Barren Island was well protected by freezing seas and Arctic conditions and had no real need of any farther defences.

He stopped abruptly as an obstacle took shape in the night, vaguely-white but too clearly outlined to be a natural ice ridge or drifted snow against a hill. He was shivering and his teeth started to chatter again but he hardly noticed them now as he moved closer. The obstacle became clearer and he realised that it was a square concrete building of approximately twenty feet square and half as high. It was painted white so that the walls were camouflaged against the snow. He could appreciate how difficult it would be to see it from the air, even in summer, and could understand what the Norwegian pilot had meant when he reported just the faint suggestion of buildings.

Carefully Larren made a circuit of the building. Nothing alarmed him, but there was also nothing to see. There were no windows, and although he found a steel door it was sealed tight and there was no glimmer of light around the edges. There was no sound from inside and nothing to show whether there might be men in there or not.

Larren stayed well out of reach of the single door, just in case it should suddenly open and spill out a squad of armed Russian soldiers, and he widened his search area in the hope of finding more of the suggested buildings. He found a second one exactly the same shape and size fifty yards way, and then a third one beyond that. He began to suspect then that these concrete shelters simply protected the entrances to some kind of research station or naval base beneath the ice.

He paused to consider the idea, and as he did so the cross hairs seen through the sight of a light but powerful rifle lined up on the centre of his back. The sniper gently gathered in the pressure on the trigger and the rifle barked. The bullet hit and Larren spun round and toppled face down in the snow.

Sixty yards away the fur-muffled sniper smiled with pleasure and lowered his rifle. He stood up and his companions followed slowly behind him as he moved towards the still body.

10

Doctor Nina

She had brown eyes, that was the first thing that Larren saw, unusually large brown eyes that gazed into his own with a concentrated stare. The lashes were dark and curling at the corners, while the brows above were lighter and finely curved. Her dark brown hair was drawn close about her head and gathered at the nape of the neck where it flared out again into an attractive swan's tail. Her face was delicate, almost fragile, lacking make-up and needing none. She wore a little lipstick, just enough to redden her mouth and accentuate the fine lips. She wore a crisp white coat with a row of silver-topped pencils glinting from the breast pocket, and when she saw that he had recovered consciousness she gave him a warming smile. Larren wondered who she was, and what had happened to

154

him, and then she straightened up from his bed and he saw the hard-faced soldier beside her. The man was pointing a sten gun directly at his head.

Larren moved his head and pain jumped instantly into his skull. He remembered the Blenheim crashing down through the Arctic night and his harness snapping to pitch him against the cabin window, and thought that this must be Doctor Margaret. Then he remembered that he had woken up once before and that Margaret Norstadt's eyes were silver-grey, and her hair was yellow.

The woman bent over him again and spoke quietly. The words were strange but somehow he knew that they were Russian. The rest of his memory spurted back at him then; the ordeal of crossing the straits, Barren Island, and the mystery concrete buildings. There had been the crack of a shot and a great fist had snapped tight over his brain, blotting out everything in the crushing blackness.

He waited for the ache in his head to subside a little, and then asked, "Who are you?"

Almost automatically the sten gun jabbed to within six inches of his face. The woman looked angrily at the scowling guard and pushed the weapon away again with her hand.

"So you are English," she said quietly. "We rather thought that you would be. I am Doctor Nina Petrovitch, Lieutenant-Surgeon of the Soviet Navy. But who are you?"

"I'm not really sure." Larren spoke warily because he had not yet decided what kind of answers to adopt. "My head aches," he explained.

The doctor smiled. "That is not surprising. When you fell you hit your head upon the side of the building and opened up an old cut that had not yet healed. You also have two nasty wounds across the upper ribs and along the inside of your arm where the bullet passed beneath your armpit. They bled badly but are not too serious. I think that you were lucky there, for although Lieutenant Malik may be an impetuous young officer, he is usually an excellent shot."

"Lieutenant Malik?"

"Yes. The officer in command of the patrol that spotted you sneaking round the outer guardroom. He should have arrested you instead of shooting at you. No doubt he will be reprimanded."

"How sad," said Larren mildly. "Convey my condolences to Lieutenant Malik."

She looked at him as though uncertain whether to be annoyed or not, and then the Russian soldier brought attention to himself again by making another jabbing movement with the sten gun and barking in his own language. The doctor looked at him sharply and snapped a reply. The man argued for a moment and then fell into sullen silence.

Doctor Nina turned back to Larren. "He does not like it because he cannot understand what we are saying. He thinks that you should be told nothing and be forced to remain silent until Major Kerensky gets here." The sten gun was close to Larren's face again and although she made a second attempt to push it away the man remained unmovable. "I am sorry about this," she apologised.

157

"But the fool seems to think that his silly gun is necessary. The members of our security division are always bloated with their own importance."

Larren made no answer for he was slowly taking stock of his position. He was lying on an examining couch in an exceedingly well-equipped surgery, and he had no doubt that he was somewhere below the square concrete buildings that she had referred to as outer guard-houses. The very size of the room and the wide range of surgical and dental instruments and equipment that entered his field of vision told him that the base they served must be of considerable size, and he realised that there must be a whole maze of underground corridors and rooms beneath the ice of Barren Island. But there was nothing that gave a clue as to its purpose. Perhaps it *was* a submarine base, but that seemed too easy an explanation, and Larren was inclined to believe that the submarine that had appeared in the straits might have deliberately shown itself in order to create that false impression.

He tried to move and found that the whole of his left side was stiff and restricted. He looked down then and saw that his shoulders were bare and that close white bandages strapped up a good portion of his chest and his left arm. He remembered what the doctor had told him about the bullet passing beneath his armpit and guessed that it had ripped through at an angle to score the flesh in both places.

Doctor Nina said calmly, "Don't try to move. I had only just finished cleaning you up when you came back to life. Just as a matter of interest your feet were beginning to be affected by frostbite and so was the area of skin around your eyes. It was a good thing that the patrol returned from their daily circuit round the coastline in time to find you, otherwise you would probably have died out there before long. What were you doing on Barren anyway?"

Larren had had time to realise now that it hardly mattered how he answered the inevitable questions, for they would only be a formality and it was pointless to deny the obvious, but before he could answer, the door opened abruptly.

The doctor jerked round, anger flickering into her brown eyes at the sound of the intrusion. She opened her mouth with the obvious intention of uttering some curt reproof, and almost as quickly closed it again. Instead she straightened up and glared at the man who had just entered. The Russian soldier who had been guarding Larren clicked the heels of his long black boots sharply together, squaring his back and stiffly lifting his chin. But his hands never moved and the sten gun stayed rock-steady as it pointed at Larren's head.

Larren studied the new arrival who had paused after entering the door. He too wore shiny leather boots, but his uniform was sombre black and sharply cut. He wore a peaked cap and the rank-tabs of a Soviet major. He was big, arrogant, and handsome in a square, hard-faced way. He returned the doctor's gaze for a moment and then addressed his first remark to the soldier guard.

The man answered crisply and briefly.

160

Larren listened but understood nothing. He could only watch faces and try to judge from their reactions what was being said. There was a short argument between the major and the doctor, and it was plain from Nina Petrovitch's expression that she had no real hope of winning. The exchange terminated when the major simply stepped aside from the door and waited for her to leave.

Nina hesitated, and then turned to Larren. Her fragile face was drawn and angry, and an angry tremor was thrusting her breasts against the crisp white coat.

"I am very sorry," she said. "But it seems that I have no choice but to leave you to the tender mercies of Major Kerensky."

Then she turned away and walked stiffly out, slamming the door behind her.

Kerensky smiled, showing clean even teeth and looking for a moment like a grown-up version of the husky type of all-American-boy who might once have played full-back for some tough university. Then he walked across the room and seated himself comfortably on the edge of Larren's couch. He waved his hand idly and without hesitation the sten gun directed at Larren's face was removed, slapping smartly against the guard's thigh as he now stood strictly to attention. Kerensky looked up almost paternally and murmured an order. The guard relaxed.

"You've got him very well trained," Larren approved. "Can he do any other tricks?"

Kerensky looked pleased. "I'm so glad you can joke. It proves my point. Doctor Petrovitch was of the opinion that you were not yet strong enough to stand up to my questions while I argued that you were. I am afraid that our aims sometimes clash and that the doctor and I do not always agree." He paused and then added, "I am responsible for the security of this base, so perhaps you can understand *why* our aims can occasionally come into opposition."

Larren nodded. "You believe that filthy capitalism is simply people exploiting people, whereas with glorious communism it's the other way about. The doctor, of course, believes in the reverse."

Kerensky's face was blank for a moment, but then the smile came back. "Another joke — now I am sure that you are fit to stand up to interrogation. First let us not try to delude each other about what we each already know. I know that you must have come from Dog Island across the straits simply because there is nowhere else from where you could have come. By the same simple logic I know that you must be one of the two men from the aeroplane that crashed there approximately thirty-eight hours ago because there is no one else whom you could possibly be. Equally obviously your only possible reason for being here is to spy on this island, and perhaps to try and trace your predecessor — a man named Cleydon or Cleyford, or some such name." He stopped to smile and then demanded casually. "Not that it really matters, but are you Mr. Larren with the broken ribs, or Mr. Carver with the broken leg?"

"I'm Larren. And incidentally, Carver

does have a broken leg."

"Of course. I hope it heals as fast as your ribs appear to have done. The radio report that we intercepted from the doctor on Dog Island detailed the whole rib cage as being badly crushed, but Doctor Petrovitch failed to find a scratch. A most marvellous recovery."

Larren had already decided that he and Kerensky just wouldn't get along, he had disliked the man from first sight.

"I live a good, clean healthy life," he explained. "Plenty of fresh air, bed early every night, and never forget to drink my milk for real deep sleep."

Kerensky ignored him. "I had my doubts about that crash, even after I had sent a couple of men across the straits to examine the wreckage. They found the cargo that you were supposed to be flying north, exactly as they were meant to no doubt, but still it seemed too much of a coincidence. Now it seems that I was right — the crash was faked."

Larren forced a smile. "We hit a reindeer in the sky. Father Christmas was making an early test run."

It was doubtful from Kerensky's expression whether he had ever heard of Christmas. He regarded Larren clinically for a moment and then said:

"I think we must stop talking riddles. Your own activities are relatively unimportant and do not concern me very much. What I do wish to question you about is the department that sent you. Which section of the British Intelligence Service employs you? Who gives you your immediate orders? Things like that."

Larren managed another smile. "I'll concede what you already know, and I'll admit what you can just as easily guess. But apart from that you can go and kiss a monkey's — "

He broke off into a strangled scream as Kerensky calmly lifted his injured arm, flipped it high in the air and then allowed it to smack down on the couch. It was the first time that the arm had caused him any pain but now it broke into an agonising throb. Kerensky just as calmly leaned forward a second time and cuffed him lightly across his bandaged head, causing a second source of pain to shatter down from the freshly-opened gash above his temple.

When Larren was able to open his eyes again Kerensky had resumed his lounging position on the edge of the couch. His solid, squared face was blank and only the eyes had narrowed fractionally.

"Who *did* send you, Larren? There must be a few names you can tell me about."

Larren said weakly, "Nobody sent me. It's against the rules to say anything else."

"Of course, the rules of the game." Kerensky leaned forward, spreading his hand over Larren's injured arm and casually allowing it to take his full weight. "But the rules also say that when you are caught you are completely alone, and that seems very unfair. It makes you wonder if it's worth it."

Larren clenched his teeth, refusing to scream but at the same time making no effort to stop himself fainting. But Kerensky was too skilled an interrogator to allow his subject to pass out too easily. The Russian major relaxed his weight before Larren could slip completely into the only retreat of unconsciousness and cuffed his cheeks gently to bring him out of the swimming blackness.

"One name, Larren," he coaxed. "The name of the man who sent you out here. Just one name and I'll give you a rest."

"Bonaparte," Larren said weakly. "Napoleon Bonaparte. He sent me."

Kerensky had leaned closer to catch the words and now he smacked the back of his fist across Larren's mouth with a first hint of anger. The emotion was gone in a moment and he stood up from the couch and walked thoughtfully away.

Larren closed his eyes and tried to fight down the crippling pains that racked the whole of his left side. But after a few moments Kerensky spoke his name. He opened his eyes again and saw that the black-uniformed major was now standing by a gleaming white tray of Nina Petrovitch's surgical instruments, idly revolving a scalpel in his hands. He said conversationally:

"Have you ever thought, Larren, that in its own way a doctor's surgery provides an equally efficient torture chamber. These instruments for instance, which are specifically constructed to help in the curing of illness and pain, can also create pain. I think that it is perhaps this factor that causes some of Lieutenant-Surgeon Petrovitch's antagonism towards me. She feels that I defile her instruments by twisting their purpose. Consider for a moment that dental drill that stands in the corner of the surgery, normally it is only used for filling teeth after a suitable anaesthetic, but I once used it to drill a series of little holes along the bridge of a subject's nose. It was very painful for him, for I omitted to use the anaesthetic, and ultimately he talked."

He gave Larren a few moments to consider the drill and then returned to the couch. "I don't think I shall use the drill this time." His voice was still amiable. "Later perhaps, but I find the whining noise grates on my nerves."

He smiled, still toying with the surgical scalpel, and then he drew the keen edge along the bandages that bound Larren's injured arm. The top layers of white cotton parted and curled upwards, and then the scalpel pressed deeper.

"Such a shame," Kerensky said, "to undo the good work of the comrade doctor. Are you sure you cannot remember which specific department you work for? Or who sent you?"

"I remember." Larren tried to hide his fear. "It was the Moscow branch of the K.G.B. They wanted to be sure that you hadn't misappropriated the canteen tea money."

It was his last joke, for Kerensky finished severing the bandages and methodically began to experiment on the injured arm with the point of the scalpel.

11

A Sympathetic Ally?

Larren had the strange feeling that it had all happened before. The large, lustrous brown eyes were vaguely familiar, so too was the smoothly drawn hair-style with the curving, dark-brown wing-tips of the swan's tail just visible at the nape of her neck. He distinctly remembered the row of silver pencils in the top pocket of the white coat, and then, almost but not quite out of his range of vision, he saw the ugly black snout of a sten gun. He realised then that it had all happened before. This was the second time that darkness had retreated, drawing back like a slow, misty curtain to reveal the anxious face of Nina Petrovitch.

His arm burned savagely, causing a mental flash-back of Kerensky leaning over him with the scalpel while the single guard had rammed the sten gun hard into his throat to hold him down on the surgery couch. Fear trickled through him and he shifted his gaze from side to side. The same armed soldier still stood nearby, but Kerensky had gone.

"Lie still," Nina ordered quietly. "I have not finished dressing your arm."

Larren looked into the brown eyes. "It seems a waste of time. Your friend will be back."

"Perhaps." Her tone was bitter. "But I must do what I can. *God, how I hate that man*!" She stopped, as though frightened by her own outburst, and then gave a strained smile. "I have wanted to say that aloud for a long time — but I dared say it to no one here. The man is no more than a brute and an animal, but he is still the chief of the security police for this base and that makes him more powerful than the camp controller. I am sick to death of mending the bones he breaks."

Larren glanced at the statue-like soldier with the levelled sten gun. He said quietly. "I hope for your sake that you are right about this fellow not understanding English."

Nina hesitated slightly before replying, "I'm as sure as anyone can be sure of anything about the secret police. This jackal can barely speak recognisable Russian."

She was silent for a moment as she examined Larren's arm, biting her lower lip as she saw the network of cuts and gashes that now surrounded and criss-crossed the original creasing wound from the bullet.

"The swine," she said angrily. "Why did he do this? I suppose he wanted to know what you were doing on our island."

Larren shook his head. "He already knew that. I came to find a friend of mine who had vanished while trying to find out what was happening here. Kerensky wanted me to betray a few more friends."

"That is typical of Kerensky, his sole purpose is to bully people into betraying their friends. The man is an illiterate oaf. He holds his rank only because out here the ability to bluster and maintain the fear of the police is more important than intelligence." She stopped suddenly and glared at him.

"And you are a fool too for coming here. I think that perhaps you are both fools of the same kind."

"And what kind is that?"

"The kind of fool who if he is a capitalist believes that a communist must have two heads, and if he is a communist believes that a capitalist must have three."

Larren met her gaze squarely. "And what do you believe in?"

She was angry again, and this time her anger was directed at him. "I believe in people. They are all the same. They like to eat, drink, live, laugh and make love. If you cut a Moscow commissar he bleeds the same coloured blood as an American negro. Only politics are different. And politics are forced upon the people by louts like Kerensky, or by oily-tongued politicians employing spies like you."

Larren summoned a smile that only just registered around his lips. "I can't argue with that, but don't you agree that as long as there are people like Kerensky and me we should attempt to keep each

173

other under control."

Nina didn't answer, for the silent guard suddenly decided to remind them of his presence. His words were harsh and abrupt and he made a threatening movement with the sten gun. Nina turned on him savagely with an outburst that should have made him flinch. The guard listened but nothing showed on his stolid face, and when she had finished he kept his mouth closed and switched his cold eyes on to Larren instead of the doctor.

Nina turned her attention back to her patient and resumed English. "The fool insists again that if we cannot talk in Russian then we must not talk at all. I ask him how am I expected to treat a patient if I cannot speak to him." There were tiny white patches of rage at the corners of her mouth and she went on. "All this stupidity infuriates me. He says that I may be planning to help you to escape, but even if I wanted to do anything so foolish there is nothing I could do — and there is no way in which you could leave Barren even if you did escape. It makes all this suspicion so senseless."

Larren said nothing, and for the next few minutes he gritted his teeth in silence as she finished dressing his injured arm. He saw a slight smile cross the face of the watching soldier and wondered how long it would be before Kerensky came in to tear the bandages off again. Despite himself he had to admit that the added psychological torture of passing a suspect back and forth between sympathetic doctor and sadistic interrogator was pretty good, and he wondered how long he could last out.

Nina finished dressing his arm and said grimly, "It will be very sore, but it will heal if Kerensky will leave it alone. Try and sit up now and I will help you into your shirt and jacket."

Larren did as he was told and she helped him into a sitting position. He felt weak and his arm was still throbbing but apart from that he did not feel too badly handicapped. At least he appeared to be still mobile. Nina helped him to dress and as she did so he glanced towards the door, expecting Kerensky to enter at any moment. But the door remained closed and there was no reappearance of the black-uniformed Major.

At last Nina fixed a sling for his injured arm and buttoned his coat around it. Then she stepped back and instructed him to stand up. Larren did so slowly, steadying himself with his right hand. His feet were stiff and suddenly became the centre of attack for a thousand stabbing pin-pricks that almost made him crumple at the knees. Then after a few moments he was able to stand unaided. Now that he was upright Nina Petrovitch was not much taller than his chin.

She looked up at him and smiled. "I was afraid that you might not be able to walk, your feet had suffered so badly from the cold. But I think now that you will be all right." Her smile faded and she added, "And now you must go to a cell. It is Major Kerensky's orders. I wanted to keep you in the surgery but he refuses. You must keep your arm still and tomorrow I will send for you again and change the dressing." She turned and spoke to the guard.

The armed soldier nodded and raised his voice, and almost immediately the surgery door opened. Larren's stomach seemed to twist sideways and drop, but it was only another guard who appeared and not Kerensky.

Nina said, "These two will escort you." She hesitated for a moment and then went on, "I do not know what your future will be, for that is out of my hands. Most probably you will be tried as a spy. Perhaps you will be shot. But I will speak to the base controller and ask him to restrain Kerensky from re-opening your wounds. I dare not say much, but the controller is at least human. I will try."

Larren thanked her. He was unsure now whether he would be subjected to another torture session the moment he left the surgery, or whether he was to be granted a respite in the hope that Nina Petrovitch could win him over on a diet of sympathy. He knew full well that more information could be sometimes gained with the velvet glove than could be battered out with the iron fist.

He turned away from the doctor and

the two soldiers arranged themselves on either side of him. The man who had stood watch inside the surgery motioned him towards the door with a sharp prod from his sten. Larren started to move and in the same moment caught a glimpse of Nina's face reflected in the mirror-like side of a deep surgical tray. Although his back was now towards her the doctor's mouth had again paled with compressed anger as she watched his guards usher him away.

Larren left the surgery with that reflected memory in mind and for one crazy moment wondered whether it was just possible that the doctor could be sincere. Every shred of training and instinct screamed to the contrary, but the flicker of doubt was there.

Then almost immediately the problem resolved itself. It did not matter whether Nina Petrovitch was sincere or not, for either way he dared not take any risks. The only safe way was to trust no one.

He walked slowly, limping slightly between his two guards. They led him down a bare, steel-walled corridor, a square tunnel coloured a light shade of green except for inset doors of white. The corridor ended at sliding doors which parted at the press of a button to reveal a lift cage. Larren was ushered inside.

He counted three levels as the lift went down, filing the knowledge automatically and without thinking. On the third level the lift stopped. Two more armed guards were waiting in the corridor outside and his original escort handed him over with an exchange of orders.

The lift returned and one of the relief guards uttered a curt sentence in Russian.

Larren said sourly, "I love you too."

The guard copied his predecessor and reverted to simply prodding with his sten gun. Larren moved on down the corridor.

After a dozen paces he was turned left into an even narrower corridor, a mere four feet wide. Here the steel walls were painted a chill grey. The corridor was only a short one and there were three formidable-looking steel doors on each side. Larren's new guards halted him outside the last door on the left.

Larren waited while the door was opened, and then one of the guards snapped another order in Russian and indicated that he was to get inside. Larren limped slowly into the cell and immediately the door clanged to behind him. The sound had a very sharp and final note that seemed to echo again and again through his head. There was no light in the cell except for a small, criss-crossed square that passed through an eye-level grille in the door from the coldly lit corridor.

Larren heard the two soldiers outside moving away, and he wondered how long he had got before Kerensky sent for him again.

Then abruptly a figure moved in the deeper darkness of the cell.

"Simon Larren!" A calm, well-cultured voice said slowly. "I might have known that you would be the one to come after me."

Larren blinked as the man emerged into the gloom, and then he recognised the slim, ballet-dancer figure of Adrian Cleyton.

12

Strange Reunion

Cleyton showed no signs of ill-treatment and looked remarkably fit. He still wore his own clothes, dark trousers and a heavy, black, woollen sweater which had helped to conceal him so effectively in the darkness. His hair, as always, was perfectly tidy. Even in the gloom it was possible to see that his eyes were an almost limpid brown with fine, curling lashes. When he wanted them to, Cleyton could make those eyes look insipid, at other times they became as hard as Larren's own. Now they hardened as he saw that Larren's arm was in a sling.

He said quietly, "I hope that's not as serious as it looks." As he spoke he raised his left hand as though to smooth back his hair and deftly touched his fingers to his lips and his ear in passing. The warning was not strictly necessary for Larren had already guessed that there must be a concealed microphone somewhere in the cell. Kerensky would not have put them together otherwise.

The first reaction of finding Cleyton unexpectedly alive began to pass and Larren said slowly:

"It could be worse. Only a crease but a certain Major Kerensky had a little fun with it."

"Then you'd better sit down. I know the form Kerensky's amusement takes."

Larren allowed the slim man to lead him over to one of the two drab cots that were fitted against the bare wall and sat down with mixed feelings. He had written Cleyton off as dead way back in Smith's office.

"I'm sorry that the luxury standard isn't quite up to the quality of the Ritz," Cleyton said sadly. "But that's what comes of booking with an inferior travel agent. The room is terrible, the service is sloppy, and I'm not sure whether the television is working."

Larren didn't look round, but he too was wondering whether the television was working. Obviously their conversation was being overheard — but were they being watched?

He said at last, "Excuse the slow reactions, Cleyt. But up to two minutes ago I had been fully convinced that you must be buried somewhere underneath the ice, or else drifting near the bottom of the sea."

Cleyton grinned wryly. "That's where I thought I was headed when it happened. One of the Lapps from Dog attacked me in the middle of a blizzard. Took me completely by surprise. The last thing I remembered was this charming fellow standing over me with his spear aimed at my throat and then I blacked out. When I came round I was here. It turned out that my blood-hungry little playmate had a Russian patrol just behind him. They took his spear away just in time. It seems that the idea was to take me alive. I've no idea why."

He shrugged his shoulders expressively and then sat down beside Larren on the cot. "How did they catch you, Simon?"

Larren told him. Kerensky already

knew the full story of how he had crash-landed on Dog and then crossed to Barren, so the fact that the security major was undoubtedly listening to them from a tape recording somewhere made little difference. While he talked he felt Cleyton touch his wrist as they sat half-facing each other on the low cot. Cleyton's fingers moved like those of a doctor checking the rate of a pulse-beat, but instead of remaining steady they began to squeeze and relax with gentle pressure. The slim man's face was attentive but revealed no other expression. Larren continued talking and began to wonder whether Cleyton had turned slightly crazy in his solitary confinement or whether he was merely attempting to get amorous. Then abruptly he realised that the intervals of pressure were varied, some long and some short. Cleyton was taking no chances on a hidden television camera and was communicating with a simple morse code.

Larren talked and painstakingly Cleyton spelled out a brief message.

'A.n.y. h.o.p.e. f.r.o.m. C.a.r.v.e.r.?'

Larren made a slight negative motion of his head. He managed to include the fact that Carver had genuinely broken his leg a second time into his narrative and Cleyton understood.

Larren carried on with his story, making it as lengthy as possible. The pressure of Cleyton's fingertips began to spell out more letters.

'I.f. e.s.c.a.p.e. p.o.s.s.i.b.l.e. i.n.f.o.r.m. S. p.u.r.p.o.s.e. o.f. b.a.s.e. p.a.r.a.l.l.e.l.s. a.u.t.e.c.'

For a few moments the sentence spelled nothing to Larren, and then he realised abruptly that autec was not a word but a set of initials. The fact that Cleyton had been forced to spell them out letter by letter had fooled him.

A.U.T.E.C. stood for Atlantic Underwater Test Evaluation Centre, and comprised a large section of ocean with its headquarters at Andross Island in the Bahamas. It was used jointly by Britain and the United States for testing the latest devices in undersea warfare, including new developments in detecting submarines at increasing ranges, improved communication methods, and the trial firings of nuclear sub-to-sub torpedoes for arming the hunter-killer submarines that would be allotted the task of tracking down their missile-carrying opposite numbers in the event of a third world war.

While Larren's thoughts raced he continued to tell how he had crossed the straits to Barren Island in Margaret Norstadt's silver-blue cockleshell. He talked automatically and knew that Cleyton wasn't listening. Nobody was listening except Kerensky. Cleyton's fingers were pressing at his wrist again.

'F.i.s.h. o.n. D.o.g. k.i.l.l.e.d. b.y. s.o.m.e. t.y.p.e. o.f. n.e.w. s.u.b. m.i.s.s.i.l.e. — b.e.l.i.e.v.e. b.a.s.e. a.l.s.o. c.o.n.t.a.i.n.s. l.i.s.t.e.n.i.n.g. e.q.u.i.p.m.e.n.t. t.o. d.e.t.e.c.t. w.e.s.t.e.r.n. t.e.s.t.s. — i.e. s.e.i.s.m.o.g.r.a.p.h. o.n. a.r.c.t.i.c. s.e.a.b.e.d.'

Larren had to rake back into his memory to recall what a seismograph was. Then the right compartment clicked open. A seismograph was the device used to measure shock waves through the earth. Ordinarily it was used to record earthquakes, but more recently advanced ultra-sensitive models had been evolved for the purpose of registering the man-made earthquakes — namely nuclear tests. The Americans had installed one two miles deep on the seabed of the Pacific, connected by over a hundred miles of submarine cable to listening posts on the shore. The instrument was a vast step forward in the job of detecting underground and undersea explosions.

There were a thousand questions that Larren wanted to ask, but he asked the main one first. He told how he had been shot down by the unseen Lieutenant Malik as he felt for Cleyton's pulse in turn and spelt out:

'H.o.w. d.o. y.o.u. k.n.o.w.?'

Cleyton signalled back:

'K. u.n.a.w.a.r.e. t.h.a.t. I. s.p.e.a.k. R.u.s.s.i.a.n. — v.e.r.y. c.a.r.e.l.e.s.s.'

Larren would have preferred a more-detailed explanation, but there was a limit to how long they could play this game. For if they were being watched by an unseen camera then the fact that they were communicating by hand signals must register eventually, even though their cell was mostly in darkness. He continued to talk, mentioning the name of Nina Petrovitch, and then risked one final question.

'A.n.y. o.p.i.n.i.o.n. o.n. N.P.?'

The answer came slowly.

'H.a.t.e.s. K. — g.u.a.r.d.s. r.u.m.o.u.r. h.e. w.a.n.t.s. h.e.r. a.s. m.i.s.t.r.e.s.s. — N. o.n.l.y. w.o.m.a.n. o.n. b.a.s.e. — t.e.r.r.i.f.i.e.d.'

Larren pulled his wrist away then and Cleyton inclined his head slightly in acknowledgement of the fact that it was dangerous to exchange any further information. Later, Larren thought, if they leave us together.

He smiled and said wearily, "And that's it Cleyt. After the doctor had patched me up the second time two of the guards marched me down here."

Cleyton stood up and rubbed his jaw slowly. "So here we are. Any idea of what they intend to do with us?"

Larren shrugged. "Nina Petrovitch said that I'd probably be tried and shot as a spy. That probably goes for you too."

Cleyton shook his head. "I don't think so. Kerensky hinted that I was to be shipped back to Russia, and I don't think it will be to stand trial. They're not ready to leak anything about this place yet and that rules out a public trial for propaganda value. It would be quieter to have a short trial and a quick execution out here. I think that if we go to Russia it will be because there are better brain-washing facilities nearer to the Kremlin. Kerensky gave me one rough session immediately after he had picked me up, but he's left me alone since. And that's not because he's had any softening of the heart, or because he believes I have nothing to tell him. I think it's more likely because he was told to leave me alone once he had reported my capture. His bosses in Moscow will want my interrogation left to the real experts."

He looked at Larren and smiled grimly. "That will probably go for you too, Simon. He's had one little go at making you talk in the hope of earning a few personal kudos. But now he's realised that you won't crack right away he'll lay off. He won't risk a Moscow reprimand for killing you by mistake."

Larren wondered how Kerensky was reacting to this summing-up of his own character, but he knew that Cleyton was right in airing his speculations aloud. If they made it too obvious that they suspected a hidden microphone then they would be promptly separated. At the same time he couldn't help hoping that Cleyton wasn't overdoing it.

He said slowly. "I hope you're right, Cleyt. If we are sent to Russia then there's a minute hope that we might be able to make a break once we reach the mainland. As far as I can see we'd have about as much chance of getting out of hell as we have of getting off this island."

"And in the meantime?" Cleyton queried morosely.

"In the meantime I'm going to get some sleep. My head aches too damned much for any more thinking."

* * *

But Larren didn't sleep. His head was throbbing dully as he claimed, and so was his left arm. But he lay on his back on the low cot with his eyes closed and the injured arm folded across his chest and continued to think. His thoughts revolved like cats chasing their own tails and despite the pain in his skull he had to try and catch them and straighten them out.

He was uneasy about everything that Cleyton had told him. Every fact seemed to fit too neatly into the picture, but then when he turned them round they failed to fit at all. The explanation that the base was the headquarters for a parallel programme to A.U.T.E.C. seemed quite plausible. The field of undersea warfare was quite obviously going to be an important one if the conflicting powers of east and west ever did cease their political arguing and come to actual blows, and it was quite feasible that the Russians would want to investigate every facet of that field as thoroughly as the west were doing. The testing of sub-to-sub missiles adequately answered the mystery of the shoal of radio-active fish that had been washed up on Barren Island, and also explained the presence of the submarine that had reared up out of the straits to frighten the Dog Eskimoes. Everything in fact fitted. Except for one thing. The Americans and the British were going about their programme quite openly, there was a tight security clamp on details and findings but the broad purpose of A.U.T.E.C. had even been reported in the newspapers. Why then were the Russians so insistent upon absolute secrecy for their own project? Why too had they installed the headquarters for their testing centre here on Barren, practically on the doorstep of pro-Western Norway, when they could so easily have used one of their already constructed submarine bases along their own Siberian coastline?

The more Larren thought the less happy he became. He began to wonder whether it was possible that Kerensky was not so unaware as he appeared to be of Cleyton's ability to understand Russian.

There was a possibility that the security major had been deliberately dropping stray tit-bits of false information.

Then a second possibility suddenly hit him. How much could he really trust Adrian Cleyton?

He repelled the thought almost as quickly, he had worked with Cleyton in Athens, and twice Cleyton had saved his life. Besides, Smith rated the slim man as one of his best agents, and Smith was not the man to make that kind of mistake — he couldn't afford them. Cleyton had to be straight.

Then slowly the doubt began to creep back again. How far could anyone trust anyone in this business? International espionage brewed more double agents than leaves that fell in autumn. His mind went back to Greece and the island of Kyros in the Aegean Sea. The job, the recovery of a vital drug antidote, had been one of the few that did not involve direct entanglement with any branch of Communist intelligence. An ideal job in which a double agent could happily shine.

Carefully Larren opened his eyes. The cell was still in darkness, but Cleyton was standing against the wall close to the chequered slit of light that came through the barred grille. His arms were folded across his chest and he was staring blankly, as though deep in thought, at the point where the floor vanished beneath the wall on the far side of the room. Even in his thick sweater he still looked tall and slim, and Larren found himself thinking again how remarkably fit he looked. He had talked of one rough session with Kerensky, but there were no visible marks on him.

Larren closed his eyes again and fought back the horrible aching of his head. If anyone else had suggested to him that Cleyton might be a double agent he would have refused to believe it. He didn't want to believe it. But was it possible?

He wanted to reject the idea completely, but he couldn't reject the fact that Cleyton knew too much with too little an explanation. It just did not seem feasible that he would be allowed to overhear enough scraps of information to piece his knowledge together. Even if Kerensky did believe him to be ignorant of Russian it was highly unlikely that the security man would take any risks.

Then a new answer occurred, equally unpleasant but more acceptable. In the past the Russians had successfully brainwashed many of the captured agents who had fallen into their hands. Brainwashing was almost rated as one of the main Communist industries. Could Cleyton have succumbed to some new line of short-term treatment? He stayed with the thought for a few moments and then decided that it was impossible. Cleyton had only been in Russian hands for a matter of five days, and no short-term brain-washing process could be quite that short. It was a job that normally would take several months.

He harried the problem until his head felt fit to burst, and at the end he had only three possible answers.

Either Kerensky's security was lax up here in the Arctic and Cleyton had managed to grasp the basic principles of what was going on simply by understanding Russian when he was believed to be ignorant of the language.

Or Kerensky had fooled Cleyton completely.

Or Cleyton was working with the Russians and they were all attempting to fool him.

The last two possibilities raised the stumbling block of why should the Russians even bother to feed them false information when they could quite simply be shot out of hand.

He finally gave up thinking and tried to sleep, for his headache had increased to the proportions where sleep was his only escape. His thinking was completely confused and he knew it would get him nowhere until his brain had cleared. He simply had to sleep.

★ ★ ★

He was awakened by the clang of the door slamming back, and he still had his headache. He struggled up slowly, feeling a twinge of pain as he inadvertently started to use his injured arm.

Two Russian soldiers stood in the cell doorway, both of them holding stens. Adrian Cleyton sat upright on the second cot and started to get to his feet. One of the sten guns sharply motioned him back again. The second sten was levelled at Larren and indicated with a jerking movement that he was to get up.

Larren climbed to his feet. He realised grimly that he had made a mistake in attempting to sleep, Kerensky had watched him settle down and then chosen that moment in which to wake him, and he had little doubt of what the Soviet major wanted.

He moved slowly towards the door and his arm began to throb in anticipation.

13

A Wild Gamble

For once Larren's fears were groundless.
He was not taken to Kerensky to
continue his interrogation but was simply
transferred to an empty cell farther up
the corridor. The two soldiers waved him
inside and one of them even relaxed
far enough to smile. No doubt he had
guessed the lines of Larren's thinking.
The door slammed behind him and then
Larren was alone.

He wondered why.

Why had they first put him in with
Cleyton and then separated them? The
obvious reason was that Kerensky had
hoped to pick up something from their
conversation, but then given up when
he realised that they suspected a hidden
microphone. But Larren distrusted obvious
reasons. In fact, he realised bitterly
that he was fast beginning to distrust

everything — and everybody. He was looking for subtle, hidden motives in everything that happened and succeeding only in accentuating his headache.

He finally walked over to the low cot against the wall, for this cell was identical to the one he had just left, and carefully stretched himself out. He wondered whether he would again be instantly awakened as soon as sleep washed over him, and then deliberately concentrated on making his mind a blank.

* * *

He awoke naturally, experiencing first surprise and then uneasiness. He hadn't expected them to allow him to rest and he wasn't fully happy with the unexpected. The pattern was all wrong. There should have been flashing lights in his eyes, an endless convoy of interrogators, threats and promises, no rest and no sleep, the temperature treatment, hot baths and cold baths, kicks and blows and no clothes. Instead there was nothing, and he didn't really like it.

What the hell were they playing at? Was Cleyton right in believing that Kerensky had been ordered to leave them unharmed until they could be transported home to the genuine experts in mother Moscow?

He lay still on his bed and continued to relax, pondering quietly. He tested his injured arm by raising it above his chest and received an immediate twinge, but when he kept it still he could almost forget about it. His head had once more improved almost to normal and he wondered how many hours he had slept. He was still wondering half an hour later when he heard the guards outside his cell.

A key turned and the cell door slammed right back. Larren guessed that it must be a routine precaution to kick the door right back against the wall before entering, that way they could not be surprised by anyone hiding behind the door. He started to get up but the inevitable sten gun waved him back. The second guard placed a tray on the floor and then they both retreated and the door slammed shut again. Larren noted that they were not the same two soldiers who had put him here and reasoned that he had slept long enough for the guard to change.

He got up slowly and inspected the tray in the brief square of falling light from the inspection slit. The tray was about a foot square and made of thin plastic, not half heavy enough for hitting anybody over the head. It held a plastic jug full of black coffee, again nowhere near heavy enough for hitting purposes, one paper cup, three crisp rolls of white bread, a large paper plate full of stew and a small plastic spoon.

Larren breathed in some of the stew aroma and suddenly realised that he was ravenous. He picked up the tray and returned to his cot, resting the tray on his knees. He ate two rolls and three parts of the stew before it occurred to him that they might be doped.

He hesitated, and then began to eat again. If he didn't eat what the Russians gave him then he would starve, and it was too late to start worrying now anyway. Besides the stew tasted good. When he had finished he toyed idly with his little plastic spoon. A real hero would use this to stab the guard in the eye as he collects the tray, he thought cheerfully, but I'll wait for something more foolproof to come along. The food had strengthened him and restored his spirits and he replaced the tray on the floor and then returned to his cot and his thinking.

The tray was collected some twenty minutes later. Larren lay on his cot and watched the operation without comment. When the door was shut upon him once more he resumed his meditations.

Despite the fact that the food and the rest had cleared his head they had done nothing to clear his thoughts. He passed a mental comb through all the possibilities and question marks of yesterday — or perhaps it was the day before, or earlier this morning — but still he was unable to reach any satisfactory conclusions. It was like playing blind man's buff inside his own brain.

Finally he boiled the problem down to one basic issue. The need to escape. If he could only get his report to Smith then that deceptive little man with the razor brain would stand a much better chance of sifting fact from fiction. Larren knew that one man in the field rarely uncovered the complete answers to any intrigue. Instead the final picture was usually built up in Smith's offices after consultation with a flock of experts and the cross-checking of reports from dozens of working agents. The specks of truth were separated from a sea of red herrings, and perhaps somewhere in that particular sea that swam endlessly in his own brain was the particular speck of truth that Smith needed. His job was not to classify what he had learned, but to get it all back to the trained brains of the department.

He felt better for having reached one solid issue and began to take more interest in his cell. One thing he would badly need to know if escape was to be attempted was whether or not he was being both taped and watched as he believed he had been in Cleyton's cell. His eyes were fully accustomed to the darkness now and he began to carefully search the ceiling and the walls for any tiny aperture that could indicate the presence of a camera.

He couldn't find one — which meant that he still didn't know. For in the near darkness at the back of his cell he could easily have missed it. He hesitated and then left his cot to search properly, running his fingers over every inch of the wall. He couldn't quite reach the ceiling but he studied it until his eyes ached. Finally he went back to his cot and relaxed again, thankfully closing his eyes. He thought that it was still most probable that there was a microphone, for it would be undetectable under a thin layer of plaster and mikes were almost a standard fitting in any Communist prison cell, but he was eighty-five per cent sure that there was no camera. He had to be satisfied with that.

After several hours another meal was brought in to him, again on the feather-weight tray. There was more black coffee and rolls, and this time some cheese and butter. He ate dubiously but the food was good. It still puzzled him.

The tray was taken away and he was

left to his own devices again, which consisted of more dead-end thinking. Once he got up and peered through the grille, and was able to see along the narrow corridor to Cleyton's cell three doors away on the opposite side. But there was no way of telling whether the slim man was still confined there or not. Larren returned to his bed and sat down.

He was still sitting there when the door opened again, and this time the first butterfly was flitting into his stomach even before he saw that the guards were empty-handed except for their stens, for it was too soon for their arrival to herald another meal. This time one of the guards had been replaced by an N.C.O. and it was he who barked the order that unmistakably meant that Larren was to leave his cell.

Larren walked out into the corridor and the two soldiers marched him back to the main corridor and thence to the lift. Larren noted that the soldier who had brought his meals was relaxing in a small room just off the main corridor and guessed that this must be the guardroom. As far as he could see the two men and their N.C.O. made up the complete guard, and even though that seemed adequate here under the ice where escape seemed pretty hopeless anyway, Larren filed the knowledge away.

He was prodded methodically into the lift and again he counted three levels as the lift rose up. When it stopped he found himself back in the corridor that led to Nina Petrovitch's surgery. He remembered Kerensky's comments upon the similarity between a surgery and a torture chamber and a swarm of locusts joined the butterflies that already danced beneath his belt. His escorts paraded him in front of the surgery door and knocked.

It was the doctor's voice that answered.

Larren still expected to find Kerensky awaiting him, but Nina was alone except for the sour-faced soldier whom he remembered from the first time he had found himself in the surgery. His escorts from the cell block stayed outside, but he was immediately under the threat of the sour-faced man's gun.

Doctor Nina smiled at him and said calmly, "Come right in, Larren — you see I know your name now. I hope they have not been treating you too badly."

She was sitting behind her desk and Larren took the indicated seat opposite her. The guard stood with his back to the door.

Larren said slowly, "Better than I expected, I must admit. I haven't yet received another visit from Kerensky, and that surprises me."

Nina smiled again, and managed to look more feminine than professional despite her crisp white coat. "It almost surprises me also, but I can explain it. I told the base controller that I could not be responsible for your health if Kerensky continued to tear off every dressing I applied. I think that ensured you a little better treatment, although it has also increased Kerensky's antagonism towards me."

Larren's doubts began to filter through his mind again as he listened to her. Was it possible that she and Kerensky really were enemies? Cleyton had said that Nina was the only woman on the base and that Kerensky wanted to make her his mistress, which could well be true. Nina Petrovitch was a very attractive woman, and stripped of that white coat and whatever else she might wear beneath it he did not doubt that she would be more attractive still. Even in crowded London or Moscow she would still be a very bed-worthy proposition. Here in the Arctic, to a man like Kerensky to whom sex was undoubtedly a necessity, she would be a constant source of desire.

He answered her while his mind was still working. "Why do you concern yourself over me, Doctor? Considering that you regard me as a spy who will ultimately be shot in any case."

"Because — " Her voice hardened a little. " — I am a doctor, and you are my patient. I believe that in your country a doctor takes an oath to do his best for all patients, whether they be murderers, prime ministers, or spies. A Russian doctor is not all that different, contrary to all your propaganda." She stood up, and finished curtly, "Now I will attend to your arm."

Larren waited for her to circle the desk. There was a hint of suppressed anger underlying her movements and he began to feel instinctively that she was genuinely interested only in her work, that perhaps she did detest Kerensky and was disgusted by politics. But the situation was now so tangled that he did not trust his instincts. He preferred to believe that she was still attempting to win him over with the velvet glove, because that way he could make no mistakes.

He stood up as she came round the desk and she helped him off with his jacket, hanging it on the back of his chair.

"How does the arm feel?" she asked as she began to unbutton his shirt.

"Stiff," he replied. "And a little bit sore." He helped her as much as he could and then winced as she started on the bandages that were taped around his upper arm. Her expression had become professional as she worked and she did not look up. Larren studied the top of her head for a moment, resisting the temptation to stroke his free hand over her smooth, dark brown hair where it spread out into that luxurious swan's tail at the nape of her neck, and then his gaze roamed further afield.

Then he saw the scalpel.

The keen silver blade was almost hidden by a flat desk calendar that lay almost within arm's reach. It looked identical to the instrument Kerensky had used upon his arm and only a gleam of reflected light from the desk lamp made it visible. For a fraction of a second he stared at it and then he snapped his gaze away. The armed soldier was still watching him intently from the door a few paces away, but appeared to have noticed nothing.

Larren's mind accelerated. He had only to lean forward swiftly and scoop up the scalpel — but then what? Nothing except be cut to pieces by the guard's sten. But his jacket was hanging on the chair-back with its pocket gaping open immediately under the front edge of the desk. If he could get the scalpel into that pocket then at least he could leave here with a weapon. The scalpel would be a very good substitute for a knife, and Simon Larren was as deadly with a knife as any man alive. In the dark he would as soon have a knife in his hand as an army at his back.

He risked a sideways glance at the guard and saw that for the moment the man's eyes were resting appreciatively on the doctor, and Nina was blocking his view of the half-hidden scalpel. The bandages were pulling at Larren's skin now as she unwound the last few inches, and he realised abruptly that here was one chance to move and get away with it.

He waited until she gently tugged at the large lint pad that had been pressed to the wound itself and then gave a sudden wincing yelp and jerked his body away. The movement sent an arrow of fire up his arm that made his yell of pain genuine at least as the pad was ripped off, but it also brought him close against the large desk. His right hand slapped down on the desk calendar and swept both calendar and scalpel to the edge of the desk. Almost instantaneously the hand swept up again to clutch at his injured arm just below the mutilated bullet wound.

Nina was staring at his face but the guard instantly started to move forward.

"You damned fool," Nina said angrily. "It wouldn't have hurt half so much if you hadn't pulled away."

"I'm sorry," Larren apologised weakly. He didn't dare look at the guard and felt absolutely sure that the man was still moving towards him. It had been a crazy move and the man must have seen or guessed what had happened. He tensed for the savage blow from the sten gun that must at any moment knock him aside and went on desperately, "You caught me by surprise. It hurt suddenly when I wasn't expecting it."

"Let me see." She pushed his right hand away and lifted his arm slightly to inspect it. "You only made yourself shout," she said. "You haven't done any damage."

Larren forced himself to breathe normally, and another thirty seconds passed before he dared risk another sideways glance at the guard. The man had only made that one instinctive movement and then relaxed. Now he was smiling sardonically.

Larren wished that he too could relax and smile, but he knew that he must carry on with what he had started. As Nina began to fix a fresh dressing to his arm he let his right hand rest on the edge of the desk as though to steady himself. After a moment he stretched his fingers and touched the edge of the calendar pad. He winced slightly and covered another move, and then part of the pad and the cold touch of the scalpel were both under his hand.

The guard was watching him, but Larren's own body was shielding his movements now. He only wanted the guard to look away for a single second and he could drop the scalpel into the open pocket of his jacket.

The guard stared at him woodenly.

There was a dry taste in the back of Larren's throat. He didn't dare watch the guard too closely in case the man should suspect. Nina was now passing the last of the clean bandage around his arm and it was too late to feign another wincing movement, even if he had been prepared to risk the same trick a third time. Nina began to fasten the end of the bandage and Larren knew that at any second she would step back, and once she was no longer partially blocking the soldier's view then his last chance would be gone.

Nina stepped back and Larren felt suddenly naked. He waited for the guard to shout and order his hand away from the scalpel. Then Nina said calmly:

"You'd better sit down while I change that bandage on your head."

Larren had completely forgotten his head injury. He murmured a word of assent, half-turned as though to locate the chair which was already pressing against the back of his thigh, and sat down. His hand brushed the scalpel off the desk and it fell into the open pocket of the jacket without even a plop.

The guard still watched woodenly, but his expression never changed. Larren breathed an inward sigh of relief and prayed that Nina would not discover the loss of one of her surgical instruments until it was too late. It would just be foul luck if her next patient was some spotty-necked Siberian soldier with a boil to be lanced.

Nina carefully changed the bandage around his head and commented that the long gash was healing nicely. Then she helped him on again with his jacket. Larren's mouth dried again as he inserted his one good arm but she noticed nothing amiss.

She told him to sit down again and then returned to her own chair behind the desk. She wrote for a moment, filling in a report card, and then looked up. Her voice became slightly official.

"I am authorised to tell you Larren, that in a few days' time a ship will arrive to take you to Russia." Her brown eyes became fractionally hesitant and she glanced down at her report again. "I wish I had some better news to tell you, but I think you will be interrogated by the K.G.B. Meanwhile I shall see you daily while you are in my care."

She looked up again and signed to the guard by the door.

She resumed her writing as the guard called to the soldier and N.C.O. who had remained waiting in the corridor, and she didn't look up as he was escorted away. Larren's mind was moving fast and he didn't at all fancy the idea of being interrogated by the K.G.B., Russian's vicious security police. He had to escape — somehow.

As they descended towards the cell-block level he thought crazily of attacking his two-man escort in the close confines of the lift where they were unable to level their sten guns. But he knew that the idea was impossible even as it occurred, for the N.C.O. was holding his sten with the butt low and the ugly barrel angled upwards. One false move and a burst of fire would rip into the underside of Larren's chin and just about wipe his face away. The idea meant suicide.

The lift stopped and Larren thought bitterly that perhaps that was all his puny scalpel was good for, just suicide. And then the word suicide triggered off another idea. An idea that seemed equally crazy, but one that stuck, revolved, and then developed slowly in his mind.

By the time he had reached his cell he had decided that crazy as it might seem the idea could work. It all depended upon the dubious question of whether or not his cell was under camera surveillance. And on that he still wasn't quite sure.

He sat on his cot for an hour after his guards had locked him in the cell, thinking hard and again scanning the ceiling for any trace of a watching eye. He still couldn't see one and finally he decided that the only thing he could do was to gamble and take the risk. If he could have thought of any alternative use for his hard-won blade he might have deterred, but there was nothing else and it was only a matter of time before Nina Petrovitch must discover and report its loss.

He waited a while longer, until he judged that it must be nearing the time for the guards to bring him another meal. They had taken his watch away but his stomach provided him with a rough estimate of when it was time to eat.

He stood up from his cot and moved over to the light from the grille, and then for the first time removed from his pocket and examined his prize. The blade of the scalpel was razorsharp. He held it in his hand, gently, his finger and thumb gripping the end of the blade so that only a sixteenth of an inch of the cutting edge protruded.

His hand trembled slightly, and he forced himself to wait until it had steadied. Then he raised his chin, started just underneath his left ear, and slowly and carefully moved the scalpel across his own throat. The shallow cut smarted horribly and he had to clamp his teeth hard together until he had finished.

He lowered himself shakily to the floor, withdrawing his stiff left arm from its sling as he did so. He sprawled on his back with the lightly blood-stained scalpel still in his outstretched hand. He had no mirror with which to examine his own handiwork, but he lay so that the light from the inspection grille fell upon the shallow red line across his throat as his head lolled back, and he was pretty sure that in the vague light the cut that had only nicked the skin would look much deeper and more fatal.

He had only to wait for the guards to arrive.

14

Blackmail, Bribery and Threats

The time of waiting seemed interminable, but at least it assured him that the biggest risk had been non-existent. The fact that the guards had not appeared instantly was proof that there was no television camera trained on his cell. Larren had spent the first few minutes fully expecting the guards to appear in force to kick the scalpel out of his hand and then hammer home a punishment with the butts of their stens, but when they failed to appear he began to hope he could make his wild gamble pay off.

He had no idea of how long he lay sprawled on the concrete floor, but gradually cramp began to mingle with the cold that had seeped into his body. He was tempted to get up but at the same time he was sure that the guards must arrive at any moment and he dared not risk having them catch him unawares. They approached so silently that they would be almost certain to hear him move if he attempted to scramble into position at the last second. He stretched his legs as much as he was able to relieve his muscles and continued to wait.

Another age passed and he was again tempted to sit up, just for a few precious moments, and then abruptly he heard a key rattle in the cell door. Larren opened his eyes wide and stopped breathing. The guard had clearly not bothered to check through the inspection slit, for the door was slammed right back as usual before the flood of light from the corridor and the guard's startled exclamation came together.

Larren lay unmoving, not breathing, on the floor. His wide open eyes stared upwards, rolled back so that their blank gaze was fixed somewhere in the dark end of the cell.

Both guards entered his lower range of vision, staring down at the red line across his throat and the scalpel in his hand. One guard carried the meal tray, the second kept his sten pointed at Larren's motionless chest.

After that first exclamation neither guard spoke. Then the man with the sten planted his foot firmly on the inside of Larren's wrist, taking absolutely no chances as he removed the scalpel from the limp fingers. Then he leaned closer and stared hard into Larren's eyes.

Larren desperately wanted to blink. His eyes ached madly from the strain of holding that blank, rolled-up gaze.

For a few seconds the soldier remained kneeling over the Britisher's body, then slowly he relaxed his sten gun and allowed the butt to rest on the concrete floor. He looked up and spoke grimly to his companion with the meal tray. The second man nodded and hurried out of sight.

Larren knew that the vanishing soldier had been sent to fetch the N.C.O., and that he had only the barest few moments in which to act. The remaining guard looked down again and made a closer inspection of the thin red slash across his prisoner's throat, and as he bent closer his eyes suddenly narrowed with suspicion. In that instant Larren burst into blinding life.

His right hand moved in a lightning blurr that would have turned an old-time western gunman green with envy, and before the startled soldier could half-open his mouth to shout the driving fingers were buried deep around his throat. The guard went over backwards as Larren's left hand knocked the sten away and then Larren's knee drove up savagely to explode squarely in his groin. The guard would have screamed but with that iron hand locked on his throat he could only choke and dribble.

Larren knew that speed and silence were essential, and while the Russian was still helpless from that merciless blow from his knee he rested his weight on his left arm and used his right hand to yank the man's head forward and then slam it down hard on the concrete. With the second crunching smack the guard's eyes glazed over and even before the man had gone limp Larren was rolling to his feet and scooping up the fallen sten gun.

His left arm was throbbing like fury but there was no time to waste, and with the sten grasped in both hands he pressed his shoulders swiftly against the cell wall where he could see the corridor through the open doorway. The second soldier was already returning with the hurrying N.C.O.

Except for the two solid smacks when the guard's head had hit the concrete floor, Larren had tackled the first man in tigerish silence, but now he dared not risk making another sound in the cell which he was practically certain was fitted with a hidden microphone. Instead he pulled the door shut behind him and stepped boldly into the corridor.

The N.C.O. was only a yard away, his sten relaxed at arm's length by his side. Before he could blink once Larren's sten swept up in a murderous arc that cracked him across the side of the jaw and toppled him round in a spinning heap to the floor. The second soldier gaped, but he was still unarmed and Larren's sten had finished up to level directly at the region of his navel.

Larren was breathing heavily, but now that he had started his run only speed could carry him through. He said nothing but made a circular motion with the index finger of his left hand that the surviving soldier could not fail to interpret. The luckless man knew what was coming and was wincing in anticipation as he reluctantly turned round. Larren dealt him a crisp, methodical blow across the back of the skull with the sten gun that felled him beside the senseless N.C.O.

Without hesitation Larren stepped over the two fallen Russians and moved swiftly down to the main corridor. He checked the small guardroom and found it empty. The cell block keys lay on the table and he snatched them up. He returned at a run to the narrow corridor between the cells and the far end cell that held Adrian Cleyton.

He was still not sure of how much he could trust his fellow agent, but Cleyton had saved his life twice and at this stage he owed the slim man the benefit of the doubt.

He paused for a brief glance through

the inspection slit and saw Cleyton lying full length on his bunk. He was confident now that Cleyton had been wrong in believing the cells to be televised and was wary only of listening microphones. He tried two keys gingerly in the large lock and the second one caught and turned. He opened the door still without a sound, but some sixth sense must have alerted Cleyton for he looked round abruptly.

Larren raised his sten gun and pressed the short barrel like a silencing finger to his lips.

Cleyton's eyes widened, but his surprise lasted a minimum of seconds before his training took over. He gave a nod of understanding and rose slowly from his cot, soft-footing as quietly as a shadow across the cell. Larren closed the door behind him and they both moved out of hearing range.

Cleyton said helplessly, "Simon, how the — ?"

"Not now, Cleyt." Larren's voice was soft but final. "Give me a hand to get these two sleeping beauties out of their uniforms."

Cleyton grinned and nodded, his reactions were fast and he asked no more questions as they hurriedly stripped the two unconscious Russians and then changed into the stolen clothes. Cleyton was ready in a matter of minutes and he turned to help Larren who was having difficulty in getting his left arm into the sleeve of the N.C.O's jacket. The violent action of the last few minutes had aggravated the arm into an almost unbearable throbbing and he had to grit his teeth as the operation was performed.

"Where now?" Cleyton asked as he retrieved the two sten guns. "I hope to Christ you've got it all worked out."

Larren smiled grimly as he accepted one of the stens. "There's only one place that I can hope to find. The only place I've ever seen down here. And that's the doctor's surgery. Whether Nina Petrovitch wants to or not, she's going to lead us from there."

Cleyton hesitated, but before he could make any argument Larren was already on his way back to the main corridor and the slim man had no choice but to follow swiftly on his heels. They reached the lift and fortunately it was on the cell-block level. They both entered and Larren pressed the starter button.

As the lift rose smoothly Cleyton said, "Are you sure you're not making a mistake, Simon?"

Larren smiled. "Unless you know the layout of this place a damned sight better than I do that's an irrelevant question. I have no idea of how to find my way back to the surface, and apart from blundering around in circles in the hope of accidentally hitting the exit our only hope is to force Nina to help us." He held Cleyton's gaze for a moment and added, "I'm banking a lot on what you told me about her being terrified of Kerensky."

Cleyton's long lashes never flickered. "I'm pretty sure of it. I overheard the guards gossiping. Terrified might be the wrong word because she appears to have resisted his efforts to make her his mistress, and she has the courage to defy him when it concerns her patients, but she's still afraid of him."

As Cleyton finished speaking the lift reached the third floor and Larren pressed the stop button.

Larren said grimly, "Keep behind me, my uniform's a better fit than yours and if there's anyone outside it'll fool them a few seconds longer." Then the doors slid automatically open.

The corridor was empty, just a blank, square green tunnel. The two men moved swiftly away from the lift and Larren halted his companion with a sharp movement of his hand as they reached the surgery door.

He listened for a moment but there was no sound. He murmured a silent prayer for the doctor to be inside, and then a less earnest one that she would be alone. For if she had a patient, then it was only going to be unfortunate for the patient. Then he opened the door and stepped inside with the levelled sten. Cleyton followed.

Nina Petrovitch was there, and she was alone. She looked up sharply at the sound of the door opening and then started half-way to her feet, her pen slipping from startled fingers on to the report that lay on the desk before her. She saw the pointing sten guns and it was anger and not fear that sprang instantly into her lovely brown eyes. She began curtly:

"What is — ?"

"I'm sorry, Nina," Larren said flatly. "But as the Americans say, this is the way the cookie crumbles. Or, to translate it into Russian, the way the snowball melts. I'm sorry it has to be you, but there's no one else."

She stood upright. "Are you crazy, Larren? Your arm should still be in a sling. How — how did you get out of your cell?"

Larren heard Cleyton close the door behind him, and then the slim man crossed swiftly to the only other door in the surgery. He opened it, fanned the snout of his sten in a brief half-circle and then closed it again. The door had revealed only a small dispensary and was empty.

Larren said, "The arm will be all right, and I'll tell you later how we escaped from the cells. The main thing now is that you are going to guide us the rest of the way out."

Nina walked round her desk and faced him. "Don't talk like a fool. What makes you think that I would help you?"

Larren said bluntly, "The fact that now you haven't any choice. The very fact that we've come to you for help will practically condemn you in the eyes of Major Kerensky. The man hates you, and even if he believed you innocent I don't think he'd let this opportunity pass. And considering that you defied his sour-faced guard when he tried to stop you from talking to me in English, Kerensky must already know that your sympathies, to some extent, lie with me."

Her face angered. "This is ridiculous. I — "

"Is it, Nina," Larren's grey-green eyes were hard, almost ugly. "If Kerensky walked in and recaptured us now, do you really think you could convince him that you had refused to help us. Especially if Cleyton and I both swore that you had promised to co-operate if we could once get this far."

Her face paled. "This is blackmail. You wouldn't tell Kerensky such lies."

Larren shrugged. "What have I to lose?"

She stiffened, and then suddenly the anger vanished and she stared hard at his throat.

"Larren, there's blood — your neck — "

Larren raised his chin slightly. "It's nothing, just a long scratch. I feigned suicide with a scalpel I stole from your desk a few hours back. That's how I got out of my cell." He saw another advantage and pressed it home. "You'll find it hard to convince Kerensky that I took that scalpel without your knowledge. That will be another card stacked against you."

Nina looked baffled, uncertain, and the first glimmer of fear began to show in her eyes as she realised that Larren could be right.

Larren pressed on savagely. "Make no mistake, Nina. Cleyton and I will stop at nothing to get out of here, and we need your help whether you like it or not. And if we lose, you lose, because

232

Kerensky will have enough circumstantial evidence to crucify you."

Nina stared for a long time into those hard, unrelenting grey-green eyes, and then she said slowly, "What happens to me if I do help you? Even if we get away from Barren and you return to England — what happens to me?"

Larren said frankly, "I can guarantee you complete political asylum. And I can also guarantee that my superiors can fix you up with a job, a doctor's practice where you don't have to have the security police re-breaking every other limb you set. Strings can be pulled to smooth your acceptance with the British Medical Board."

Nina wavered, and then shook her head. "No, it is not possible. I could lead you as far as the outer guard-room. But I could not get you past the guards."

Larren smiled. "You told me that the patrol that shot me down was part of the daily routine. Are they out there now?"

"Yes."

"And are they in contact with the base?"

"Yes, the patrol leader carries a miniature radio-telephone. But — "

Larren said softly, "You can tell the guards that there has been an emergency call from that patrol. Tell them that one of those men out there has broken a leg and needs splints and a morphia injection on the spot. And you can tell them that we are your escort. I take it that we can rely on finding furs near the guardroom?"

"In the guardroom — yes. But I need a pass before the guards will let me through. A pass signed by the base controller or his lieutenant."

For a moment Larren was balked. Then he demanded, "How many guards?"

"Two."

"Then any kind of pass will do. Show it to them, and while they look at it, Cleyton and I will do the rest."

She looked at him helplessly. "You are crazy."

"And you have no choice." His voice was harsh again. "Either help us and escape with us — or we simply force you along with us as far as we can get and by then Kerensky will never believe you."

Nina hesitated, hopefully searching his face, and then she said wearily, "If you get back to the surface, how will you escape from the island?"

"The same way I arrived. My boat is still hidden." He was lying, for Margaret Norstadt's flimsy craft would be useless even if he could find it again, but he dared not tell her that he was gambling desperately on being able to steal something larger from the landing stage outside the guardroom.

Nina finally looked away from his face. "All right," she said bitterly. "It seems that I really do have no choice. In my desk are some pass cards. I will sign the controller's name myself. It will give you a few more seconds of time before the guards realise that the signature is a forgery."

Larren nodded in assent but watched her closely as she opened her desk drawer. She selected an official-looking document and held it out towards him. To Larren it meant nothing, but Cleyton leaned forward unnoticed to glance over her shoulder. The slim man smiled and silently nodded. Larren told Nina to go ahead and sign the pass. It didn't matter what she wrote upon it because he didn't intend the guards at the outer exit to have any chance of reading the words. When she had finished he said grimly:

"Thank you, Nina. But now we'd better get going. The guards we left unconscious in the cell block could come to at any moment and raise the alarm. We would have locked them in their own cells, but as the cells are sure to be taped for sound they would still have only to start shouting, so it would have been a waste of time."

Nina faltered, as though hoping for delay and then some last-minute reprieve, and then said resignedly:

"I had better walk first, it would not be normal if I allowed two soldiers to precede me. You must only step ahead to open doors."

Larren nodded. "Let's go."

Nina drew a breath and then walked slowly to the surgery door. Larren opened it and both he and Cleyton fell into step behind her as she turned down the corridor. She led them away from the lift, moving slowly.

"Walk faster," Larren murmured gently. "A doctor never dawdles in an emergency."

Nina's shoulders stiffened and she quickened her pace. She led them briskly to the end of the corridor and turned left into an identical steel-walled tunnel. A young Russian officer was walking equally briskly towards them.

Nina almost stopped but Larren's soft, "Keep walking," checked her just in time. The young Russian was only a dozen feet away and Larren hoped fervently that the base was too large for him to know every one of its personnel.

The officer saluted smartly and flashed a smile that might have been expected in the presence of the only woman on the base. Nina returned both the salute and the smile. The officer's gaze flickered on to Larren and he automatically saluted again. Larren's right hand held his sten, hanging stiffly at his side, but he brought his left hand up in sharp acknowledgement. The sudden jerk fired a sea of pain through his upper arm that almost made him scream aloud, but somehow he bit it down and kept his face blank. He was aware that Cleyton had saluted simultaneously and then the officer had passed on down the corridor.

Larren clenched his teeth as he lowered his arm and felt the sweat break out on his face. Cleyton spared him an anxious glance but made no comment.

They passed an open doorway where two clerks pecked industriously at their typewriters, and then a man in civilian clothes who abruptly appeared out of another doorway and hurried past them with a brief nod to the doctor. But nobody paid them any attention. Nina led them up a short flight of steps, along yet another corridor, and then stopped them outside a lift.

"The guardroom is just above," she informed them quietly.

Larren smiled. "It wasn't so hard was it? Just a simple matter of knowing which way to turn." His smile faded and he continued, "Let's get into the lift, but before we reach the top there's a final warning. Cleyton here speaks fluent Russian, so we can't fail to understand if you make any last-minute attempt to warn the guards. And if that happens this sten gun is going to rip a nasty hole around the base of your spine."

Nina stared at Cleyton. "You speak Russian?"

Cleyton smiled, and the limpid brown eyes looked sadly apologetic. He answered her in her own language.

Larren gave her no more time to think but pressed the button to open the doors of the lift. "Remember," he pressed home as the lift began to rise. "You really are in this as deeply as we are now. You've committed yourself fully by bringing us this far," Nina nodded her head, and now there was real fear in her eyes.

The lift stopped and the doors slid smoothly back.

As Nina had said there were only two men on duty in the guardroom, but both men were alert and directing their sten guns automatically towards the lift.

For a moment Larren thought that

some last-minute telephone call from below must have warned the two soldiers, but then they recognised the doctor and relaxed. Nina spoke to them calmly as she stepped out of the lift and Larren guessed that she must be telling them the hasty story he had made up for her about one of the outside patrol having broken a leg. The nearest guard smiled and nodded and then made some answer. Nina handed him the forged pass and his sten gun lowered unsuspectingly as he accepted it with his free hand. The second guard had also relaxed and half-turned away.

Larren and Clayton moved simultaneously, like two well-oiled machines operated by the press of the same button. The nearset guard stopped the butt of Larren's flashing sten gun squarely between the eyes as he bowed his head to examine the fake pass, while the second guard was slammed half-way across the room as Cleyton hit him across the back of the skull.

Nina winced painfully as the two men fell, sharply closing her eyes.

Cleyton glanced at her and said regretfully, "I don't like the rough stuff either, Doctor. But there was no other way."

Larren said nothing. Beyond the outer door lay freedom, but only as far as the icy, wind-lashed surface of Barren. And now as he stared at the door itself he could only think that it had all been too easy, much too easy. He had a horrible premonition now that there wasn't going to be any boat once they passed beyond that door into the howling Arctic night.

15

Back into the Night

It took them less than five minutes to scramble into three of the sets of furs they selected from the dozen or more that hung over the whole of one wall of the guardroom. Larren was again badly hampered by his left arm and it was Nina who was ready first and hurried to help him with his thick parka. Her face was anxious as he gritted his teeth and sweated, and he thought grimly that if he looked half as sick as he felt then she had good cause to look worried. However, she said nothing, for at this stage it was too late to turn back.

Cleyton located snow goggles and face masks and then they were ready. Larren led the way to the outer door. It opened on to a short corridor where the concrete floor was covered with snow and slush that had blown in from the actual exit.

Nina unlocked the steel exit door with a key she had taken from the guardroom desk and a blast of icy wind tore inside as Larren pulled it open.

Larren felt the cold slash right through him, as though that first gust of wind had already stripped him of his encumbering furs. For a moment he was harshly reminded of his last gruelling ordeal in crossing the straits, and then with an effort he pushed the memory behind him and plunged out into the black night. Nina followed and Cleyton closed the door.

Without hesitation Larren led the way boldly forwards in the general direction of the landing stage. It had been too much to hope that their escape would coincide with the few fleeting hours of semi-daylight, but at least there wasn't a blizzard blowing and the white landscape gave a few yards of visibility. The endless enemy, the wind, coiled itself around them in tearing embrace, and its howl effectively muffled any sounds they might have made as they crunched over the snow.

It was simple to find the landing stage for there was a well-trodden path leading directly to it. Larren was expecting to find a patrolling sentry but there was nothing to be seen in the darkness and he almost stepped off the edge of the quay before he realised that he was there. He stopped the sinisterly muffled figures of Nina and Cleyton with a curt hand signal, and then leaned forwards to peer down at the black sea. His sten was slung over his shoulder and in his right hand he carried a torch he had taken from the guardroom, but this close to the base he dared not use it.

For one terrible sinking moment he thought that his earlier premonition had proved to be fact, and that there was no boat below. And then he moved a few steps along the quay and saw a large naval launch tied up against a flight of steps cut out of the concrete. Again he had the uneasy feeling that it was all too easy, but he crushed it down. He signalled his companions closer and pointed down to the launch.

Nina looked at him incredulously, her eyes just visible behind her goggles. Then she raised a gloved hand and pulled down her face mask, pressing her face close to Larren's to make herself heard above the wind.

"It's too risky," she shouted. "There's sure to be a patrol boat at the mouth of the channel. We'll be stopped as soon as they hear the engine. Take us back to the boat that brought you here."

Larren shook his head. "My boat is useless," he yelled back. "It's this or nothing."

"But you said — "

"I lied! Now come on. If we are challenged then you'll have to bluff our way out with the same story about being called out to that patrol. Say they're on the sea-ice at the south end of the island."

He gave her no more chance to argue but headed for the flight of stone steps that led down to water level. The steps were slippery with slush and ice and all three picked their way down with utmost care. Larren jumped the intervening eighteen inches between the steps and the launch's deck, and then turned to steady the doctor as she came aboard. Cleyton dropped expertly beside them a second later.

The launch was a twenty-five footer with a single cabin just large enough to crush all three of them inside. It was fitted with a large spot-light in the bows and there was a high windshield that would give almost full protection to the pilot standing at the wheel. Larren started to move forwards but Cleyton stopped him.

"I'll handle the engine, Simon. Engines are my speciality."

Larren hesitated, and the slim man took the opportunity to shift past him and make for the wheel. The inactivity of waiting while his companion started the engine rasped at Larren's nerves and his arm began to throb more painfully, but when the engine coughed and pulsed into life a few minutes later he had to admit that he could not have been much faster. He moved up beside Cleyton at the wheel and shouted into the other's face.

"Switch that spot-light on, Cleyt. We'll need it to spot any ice floes drifting in the channel, and if that patrol boat is out there they'll know damn well something is wrong if we go roaring past in pitch darkness."

Cleyton's face was hidden but his hooded head nodded in agreement. He pressed a switch on the control panel and a brilliant beam of white light speared through the darkness from the mounting on the bows.

"Cast off!" Cleyton ordered crisply. But Larren had already discarded the forward rope and even as the order came it splashed into the freezing sea. Nina fumbled with the stern rope and that too slapped away as Cleyton opened the throttle and pulled the wheel to head the launch away from the quay-side.

White ice glittered in the beam of the searchlight as it swung across the bank of the channel, and then there was the wind-stirred sea, black and ugly in the brilliant gleam as the launch's bows headed towards the open Arctic. Larren knew that the next few seconds could prove vital and deliberately unslung his sten. Despite the bitter cold that almost froze his hand he pulled off his thick glove so that he could handle the trigger.

The launch moved slowly down the open channel and almost immediately the high bows of the stationary patrol boat appeared in the white beam of the searchlight.

Larren's body went rigid and he tightened his grip upon the sten, ignoring the numbing wind that stung through the thin nylon inner glove on his right hand. Nina stood beside him, equally tense, while Cleyton held the launch grimly on course.

The grey-black bows of the patrol boat slid past, and Larren saw that that too was fitted with a powerful search-light. Their own beam fanned over the sleek, dangerous length of almost gleaming hull and then speared into the night again. They were almost through.

Then they were challenged.

Larren couldn't see the owner of the ringing voice from the patrol boat's side, but he guessed that the man must be using a loud-hailer to shout above the noise of the wind. He half-lifted his sten in the belief that their run of luck had finally spun itself out, and then Cleyton pulled down his face mask and shouted back in flawless Russian.

The slim man cut the launch's movement to a drift as he waited for a reply, and then bellowed out another spatter of sentences that Larren couldn't understand. There was a third volley of words from the officer on the patrol boat's deck, and then Nina shouted an answer that included her own name. There was a moment's silence and then a final comment from their unseen challenger. Cleyton started the launch moving again and Larren began to breathe.

Nina said weakly, "Cleyton gave the story you made up. I had to identify myself. That was all. I think we've got away with it."

Larren nodded with approval and then fumbled his frozen hand back inside his glove. Then he moved forward to join Cleyton at the wheel.

Cleyton's hidden face turned towards him.

"So far, so good. Hey, Simon? But at

the start I didn't think it was possible."

Larren nodded in agreement and then they both had to concentrate on the handling of the launch as they heard the first of the grinding ice floes at the mouth of the cut. The black waves were building up and the wind was beginning to plaster sheets of flying spray across the windshield. The search-light cut a clear path across the rising seas and twice Cleyton veered swiftly off course to avoid a looming barrier of white ice.

Within five minutes they were out into the straits again, and back into the full fury of the Arctic seas. Larren shouted instructions and Cleyton headed the launch's bows south-west to head her back towards Stadhaven nearer the southern end of Dog. They were running with the seas following and the launch fairly flew through the water. Larren watched the great black, spray-streaming walls of water rising up behind them and straining to reach their stern as they crashed down and felt fear clamouring in his belly. The last time he had ventured on these hellish waters he had almost frozen to death, and the memory was like a rising tide that could not be kept down.

Then Nina pulled fiercely at his sound arm.

"Simon!" It was the first time she had ever used his christian name and she had to yell above the buffeting of the wind. "Simon, come into the cabin. There's no need for two of you to stay up here. Cleyton can hold the wheel."

The slim man looked round, for strangely his lithe slimness was evident even in his bulky furs.

"She's right, Simon." He too had to bellow. "There's no sense in both of us freezing at the same time. Get below and I'll call you when I've had enough."

Larren hesitated, but he knew they were talking sense, and finally he nodded his head to Cleyton and turned to cross the slippery deck to the cabin. He steadied Nina as she followed him, for the launch was sliding at an angle into a rushing black valley between the wave crests and there was a strong danger of the wind blasting them both over the side. With an effort he yanked open the cabin door and pushed the doctor down the steps, and then followed her as the wind slammed the door shut behind him with a ringing crash.

It was pitch black inside the lurching body of the launch and Larren fumbled clumsily for his stolen torch. He flashed it on and the exploring beam enabled Nina to find the cabin light switch and click it down. Light flooded down from the single bulb in the deck-head, generated by the launch's battery.

Larren slumped weakly against the bulk-head as Nina stripped off her gloves and then removed her goggles and face mask, shaking her head so that her thickly-furred hood fell back on to her shoulders out of the way. She steadied herself as the launch reeled and then moved forward and did the same for Larren. His face was sallow and strained in the yellowish light from the only bulb and he lacked the strength to resist.

She said flatly, "You'd better stay down here for the rest of the crossing. If you took the wheel you wouldn't be able to hold it and the seas would swamp us in five seconds. If Cleyton can't stick it out until we reach Stadhaven then I'll have to relieve him for a few minutes."

Larren wanted to argue, but he didn't. He knew she was right.

"I suppose it's your arm." Her voice had a note of frustration. "I should imagine you've pulled the bandages out of place and started it bleeding."

Larren smiled without feeling. "I should imagine I have." She might have added that the scratch across his ribs was leaking trickles of blood all down his side and that he was feeling like death, and she would have been equally right.

She pushed his chin up with finger and thumb and studied the self-inflicted cut across his throat. She said dubiously:

"Perhaps I can do something for this. There should be a medical kit aboard somewhere."

Larren shook his head. "Don't bother, Nina. The cold has already found its way under my chin and that particular little cut is completely numb. It may as well stay that way until we reach Stadhaven."

Nina hesitated, and then nodded. Then she asked slowly, "What does happen when we reach this Norwegian island? Do we wait for a ship to come and take us off?"

"No." Larren was glad of the opportunity to talk for it kept his mind off the pain of his arm and the gnawing fear of the seas that kept the launch pitching and sliding as she chased the run of the waves. "There's a boat due within a day or two but we can't afford to wait. Kerensky is sure to send that patrol boat tearing after us as soon as he realises that we have escaped and this launch is missing."

"But — but you cannot hope to get any farther than Dog in a vessel as small as this. Not in these seas."

Larren smiled, although it cost an effort. "Don't worry, Nina. We're not dependent upon either this launch, or the ship that's due to take Margaret Norstadt off Dog Island. Somewhere, not more than a few hours from here, there's a British trawler dragging her nets. But she isn't manned by simple honest fishermen, her crew are all picked men of the Royal Navy. All they need is a bleeping signal from a compact little homing device hidden aboard that crashed plane on Dog Island, and the nets will be cut free and that trawler will move in at full speed to pick us up. It was all arranged before I left London. I have a very thorough boss."

Nina said slowly, "It is a relief to hear it. Thank you for telling me."

"A pleasure." Larren's smile was becoming more strained with every effort. "And now perhaps you can tell me something?"

The launch rolled and threw them together, Larren steadied her with his good hand with his back still braced against the bulkhead. Then when they had recovered their balance he finished bluntly:

"You can tell me what really is going on at that underground base on Barren Island?"

Nina looked at him with troubled eyes, and hesitated a long time before she answered. "I suppose it is pointless not to tell you," she said at last, and there was the faintest trace of bitterness in her tone. "If we are caught now I will be shot whether I have told you or not. The base is a listening post for an undersea testing centre."

"What kind of testing centre? What exactly are they testing?"

"I do not know all the details, I am only the doctor. I do know that the base is staffed with a lot of technical officers and civilians whose work is connected with electronics and radar, and that they are working on some kind of improved communication system between submarines at deep levels. And I know that another department is testing some type of new undersea missile for arming our submarines. There are also instruments deep under the sea, connected by cables to the base that record the force of the explosions, but again I do not know much about them." She paused. "As far as I know there is nothing sinister there that threatens your countries. It is simply a research centre."

Larren listened and had to admit that it all tallied neatly with what Cleyton had overheard, and he was almost ready to believe her. But still he wavered slightly.

"But why here?" he asked. "Why choose this part of the Arctic?"

She looked at him in surprise. "Because this is the ideal place — the only place. Our Pacific seaboard is too easily spied upon by American submarines, and to go any farther north into the Arctic Ocean means that we cannot guarantee ice-free waters. Here the main part of the ocean, away from the island itself, is reasonably clear of heavy pack-ice, while the local conditions are still bitter enough to deter stray visitors." She smiled abruptly. "Well — most stray visitors."

Larren nodded slowly as his doubts were dispelled. "Tell me one more thing, Nina. This all started when one of the Lapps vanished from Dog — have you any idea of what happened to him?"

She nodded sadly. "Exactly the same as happened to you, except that he ran away and gave the patrol more reason to shoot. They brought him in to me but he died after a few hours. The bullet had passed through his lung." She looked up. "I don't suppose he even knew what he was running away from. He must have found the outer buildings simply by accident."

The rolling launch gave another violent twist as she staggered on the crest of a wave and again they were thrown together. This time Larren dropped his sten with a clatter as he used both hands to save her. Her face came very close to his own and stayed there for a moment before she looked down at the fallen sten. Then she looked back into his eyes.

"Tell me something now, Simon. Would you — would you really have used that the way — the way you said that you would if I had betrayed you."

Larren still had his hands on her shoulders. He said slowly, "No, Nina. If you had betrayed us it would have been too late, and revenge is futile."

"I thought not," her voice was suddenly very low. "I was sure of it. But I still didn't betray you."

Larren looked deep into those large

brown eyes and read nothing but infinity. He said softly:

"Why not?"

"Because — because I couldn't help to kill a man. Back on Barren there were only the sadistic louts of Kerensky's security force, and the weaklings who crawled before them. But you fitted neither category, you were not a brute, but neither were you afraid of brutes. I can't respect your reasons for coming here, Simon, but I can respect you. In a way I think I was even glad when you forced me to come away with you."

She had made no attempt to draw back after the launch had pitched them together and now her lips were very close and slightly trembling. Larren still watched her eyes and almost irresistibly her gaze drew him forward. He kissed her hard and her eyelids slowly fell as her mouth melted and moaned softly under his own. Their heavy furs restrained them from more than a kiss, but he sensed that everything else was there and offered if ever the opportunity arose to take it.

When their lips parted she opened her

eyes and looked at him again, no longer a doctor but a woman. She released her breath with a little shudder and said simply:

"Simon, when we get to your London, will you sleep with me — at least once."

Larren had less difficulty with his present smile. "Of course, all night. And if we can get breakfast in bed, all week-end."

She answered his smile. "Now you know why I allowed you to force me to come with you. Being the only woman on a base like Barren does not mean that I can have many lovers — it means instead that I can have none without stirring up burning jealousies amongst every man who wants me. But I think that from the moment they laid you upon my couch I knew I wanted you." She finished speaking and raised her lips to be kissed again.

And in that moment they both heard Cleyton's yell of alarm from the deck.

Larren was out of the launch's cabin as fast as he could move, thrusting out into the roaring wind and freezing spray.

Cleyton gripped the wheel with one hand but his body was twisted and he was pointing back the way they had come. Larren looked over the top of the cabin roof as the launch lifted on a wave and saw the brilliant white dazzle of a second searchlight spearing across the black seas towards them.

It could only be the large patrol boat, and their escape had obviously been discovered.

Even as he stared back the pursuing boat opened fire and the first shell screamed towards them.

16

Invasion

Thirty yards astern of the launch the black crest of a wavetop erupted into a cascading mushroom of spurting water as the shell hit. The splattering sound of the impact made Larren wince and for a moment his limbs were rigid. Then the freezing wind slamming into his unprotected face shocked him back to life and he spun back to face Cleyton.

"The light!" he roared. "Cut the light!"

Cleyton reacted instantly and snapped off their own spotlight. The sea ahead was plunged into darkness that sprang up like a solid wall and the launch raced on blindly. Larren yelled at Nina to stay back in the cabin and then lurched forward to join Cleyton. The slim man was already pulling the wheel to starboard to change the launch's course.

"I'm heading straight for Dog," he

shouted. "We'll never outrun them down the coast."

Larren glanced at the huge seas that became doubly dangerous with every degree they veered off course, but he knew that Cleyton was right. They hadn't a hope of racing the patrol boat to Stadhaven and their only chance was to risk a broadside wave swamping the launch as they made for the nearest point of land. He nodded approval, hanging on to the top of the windshield with one hand while he fumbled to push his face mask and goggles back into position with the other. While he fumbled a second screaming whine sounded above the noise of the wind and another fountain of water blew upwards from the sea behind them.

The second shell had landed well to port, and for a moment Larren grasped at the flimsy hope that the cutting of their own light and the swift change of course had caused the patrol boat to lose them. But then the launch breasted another rearing wave crest and as they were flung high on the skyline the sweeping beam from the patrol boat's bows pin-pointed them once again.

The beam held them for almost six seconds and then the launch plunged down into an opening chasm of water. Cleyton yelled frantically and Larren realised almost too late that the launch's head was yawing to starboard where any second would swing her completely broadside in the trough. Already the following wave was rearing up, drawing the sea from beneath them in readiness to roll the whole Arctic Ocean over their heads in one final, crushing blow.

Desperately Larren lent his weight to the wheel, ignoring the pain of his wounded arm as he used all his strength to bring her round. Cleyton's arms were rigid, and in that moment the man with the ballet-dancer figure proved that he too was no weakling, despite his deceptive appearance. A sheeting onslaught of salt spray, already half-transformed into needles of ice, tore in a flying curtain across the boat's bows. A ton of crashing water stormed over the starboard side and surged violently across the decks, tearing at their feet as the spray lashed into their faces. And then their combined efforts swayed the balance between life and death. The launch arched upwards at the stern as though aiming straight for the bottom, and then almost immediately the stern dragged again and it was the bows that were rising, rising and riding on the crest of the wave that had so very nearly buried them.

Larren released his breath in a thankful gasp at their momentary reprieve, and before he could draw in another the sweeping searchlight of the patrol boat hit them again with fiendish accuracy. Simultaneously they heard the shrieking whistle of the third shell as it arced towards them.

The explosion came a dozen yards off their port beam. The splash was deafening and the erupting mushroom showered down in a torrential downpour of falling liquid ice. The impact slammed the launch sideways and all but turned it over. Larren hung desperately to the wheel but Cleyton slipped and his grip was torn away.

There was nothing that Larren could do for his companion and he heard Nina scream from the cabin doorway behind him as the slim man was hurled across the sloping deck. For an eternity of fear it seemed impossible that Cleyton could avoid being swept completely over the side, but in the last second the launch rocked upright again and the stout bulwark rose to stop his progress and leave him sprawling helplessly.

Nina scrambled out of the cabin to help him but Larren could do nothing as he battled alone to keep the launch from being swept under. He knew that his position was hopeless now that the gunner on the patrol boat had found his range, and had it been a matter of just Cleyton and himself he would not have hesitated to surrender. But it was not just Cleyton and himself — there was Nina Petrovitch. Nina could not hope for a stay of sentence until she had been interviewed by the K.G.B., for her there would be no breathing space in which the chance to escape might possibly occur again. The odds were that Nina would be shot out of hand, and having forced her into this position Larren preferred to run with the seas until the ultimate shell found him, rather than hand her over to Kerensky.

The whole of his left arm and shoulder was now a spreading invasion of agony and Larren knew that at any moment the sea must take control and tear the wheel out of his failing hands. He just couldn't hold it alone. And then vaguely he was aware that Cleyton had struggled to his knees and was pushing the reluctant Nina back into the flimsy refuge of the launch's cabin. Grimly Larren hung on. Cleyton was still dazed and shaken but the instinct to survive needed no conscious thought to drive him stumbling back to the wheel. Together they regained control.

The lancing beam of the searchlight was still hunting for them as the patrol boat closed in, but for a moment they were deep in another plunging valley and the slash of light swept above them. The driving thud of the pursuing boat's propellers were clearly discernible above the crash of the seas and the shriek of the wind and Larren knew that the next time the light swept back it would catch them above the waves again. And it was doubtful that the next shell would miss.

The launch started to lift out of the trough as the light swung back to meet them, and then Cleyton uttered a cry of warning.

Larren saw it in the same moment. A monstrous ice floe curtained by streaming spray and illuminated by the probing beam from the patrol boat. The launch seemed to rear above it, as though it must smash down on to that smooth glacial surface, and then both men heaved on the wheel and the wall of ice rushed past them. Simultaneously they both heard the colliding of more ice floes.

"More ice!" Cleyton yelled. "We're back into the ice pack."

His hand moved to cut the throttle but Larren knocked it away.

"Keep going," he roared. "Full speed and switch on the light. It's our only chance."

Cleyton hesitated fractionally. To switch on their own spotlight would mark their position unmistakably for the patrol boat that was practically on their heels, but it would also enable them to head at full speed into the ice pack where their small launch could command greater manoeuvring ability. The gamble lay in whether they could get out of range before the patrol boat blew them out of the water in a thousand scattering pieces. Cleyton switched on the light.

The beam from the patrol boat found them in the same second and they heard the instant scream of a shell. Their own spotlight showed ice all around them and in that moment it was impossible to swerve to either side. The sea had lost its violence, flattened by the weight of the cracked ice floes, and the launch made a perfect target in the flooding swathe of the pursuing searchlight.

Larren realised afterwards that the helmsman aboard the patrol boat must have taken sudden avoiding action to miss the large ice floe that had almost collided with the launch. It was the only explanation to the abrupt shifting of the searchlight and a complete miss that landed twenty yards away. But even the complete miss was almost fatal.

The shell hit dead centre of another large piece of floating ice and the crunching roar of the explosion was almost deafening. The ice floe was totally shattered and a murderous fusilade of flying splinters raked the launch from stem to stern, frozen knife-edges of ice that would have cut the two men to ribbons if they had not been thickly protected by their heavy furs. The biggest surviving slab reared out of the frenzied upheaval and skimmed towards them like some fantastic great white spinning top. Nina Petrovitch screamed again and Larren was certain that that deadly ice missile would rip through the stern of their launch, and then miraculously the slab of ice had passed behind them and ploughed, still spinning, into another section of the ice pack.

The launch had heeled over wildly as the force of the blast flung her to starboard, but Cleyton had fully recovered his wits and with Larren's weakening help he held her on course.

The patrol boat was dropping behind and a burst of despairing sten-gun fire followed them blindly as they sped through the scattered floes and out of range of the hunting searchlight. Their own light picked out a channel into the deepest part of the ice field, leading towards the shore, and Cleyton swung into it. Almost immediately he cut off the spotlight.

The light from the patrol boat was sweeping the cracked maze of the ice behind them as Cleyton cut the launch's speed. The white ice showed up in darkness as he drove up the narrowing channel. Larren left him to the wheel and stumbled back to the cabin. Nina looked whiter than the Arctic landscape inside her deep hood.

"Get ready to get out," he ordered grimly. "We won't have a lot of time before they lower a small boat to follow us."

He pushed her towards the deck as he spoke and grabbed up the two sten guns. Nina was almost out of the cabin and then fell sprawling as the launch reached

271

the end of its run and wedged with an abrupt jolt between the closing sides of the channel.

Larren fell flat on his face over the small table as he was jamming his torch in his pocket, but almost instantly he was up again. He slung one sten over his shoulder and used his good arm to haul Nina to her feet as he followed her out of the cabin. He chucked the second sten to Cleyton who caught it neatly with one hand as he took Nina's free arm. All three of them scrambled out on to the ice and headed inshore as fast as they could run in their heavy furs.

The next few minutes were almost as dangerous as those last moments of their escape from the patrol boat, for they moved with reckless speed across the slippery network of windswept ice floes. Twice they almost blundered into fissures of freezing black water, and once they had to turn along the edge of a deep split for several yards before it became narrow enough for them to jump. The patrol boat had inched deeper into the ice pack, but it couldn't get close enough to

272

the main mass to land any men without first lowering a smaller boat, so they had enough time to lose themselves in the bitter darkness of the Arctic night. The jungle of shifting ice with its death-trap channels of sea vanished behind them and the terrain became permanently solid. They were able to move even faster and the last faint pulse of the patrol boat's engines was blotted out by the howl of the wind.

Larren stumbled and for a moment their progress was halted.

Nina said breathlessly, "What happens now, Simon? Where's your crashed plane?"

"I've no idea," Larren said bluntly. "We'll have to get back to Stadhaven and pick up Doctor Margaret and Joe Carver. I was unconscious when I was carried out of the plane, but Margaret should be able to lead us back to it."

Cleyton faced him. His face was unreadable behind mask and goggles, but his voice was grim. "In that case we'd better hurry. The last time the wind began to build up pressure the way it's doing

273

now the weather turned into a full-scale blizzard. And I don't fancy the idea of walking through a repeat performance."

There was no arguing with the elements and immediately they hurried on, Larren leading despite the throbbing of his arm. It took them another hellish hour to cross the frozen island, and by then Nina was in need of Cleyton's steadying support. The blizzard threatened to engulf them at any moment, but still held off until Larren saw a welcome glimmer of light from the window of the medical post.

They circled the long hut, and two minutes later stumbled gratefully into the warmth of the hospital ward where an alarmed Joe Carver almost started out of bed, his hand diving for his gun.

"It's okay, Joe!" Larren pushed back his goggles and hood and clawed down his face mask as he spoke. "It's only the return of the prodigal son. Only don't kill the calf — we haven't the time."

He and Cleyton sat Nina down on the nearest bed and in the same moment Margaret Norstadt appeared in the doorway to her living quarters. She was wearing her bright red-and-orange sweater and dark slacks, and looked as completely surprised as Carver had been. The silver-grey eyes were open wide.

"Larren! We thought you were dead. You've been gone almost forty-eight — " She recognised Cleyton then and words completely failed her.

Larren smiled grimly. "Sorry to shock you, Doctor. But it's old-ghost week from now till Thursday. Everybody's coming back from the dead." He remembered the formalities and added. "Doctor Margaret Norstadt — Doctor Nina Petrovitch. The Arctic is full of ghosts and beautiful lady doctors."

Carver recovered his balance. He drew a breath and said determinedly, "Larren, what happened on Barren?"

Larren moved over to the ever-burning oil stove in the centre of the room, drawing off his gloves to warm his hands.

"There isn't time for explanations, Joe. Margaret, what time is that boat due to take us off?"

"About — about another ten hours." Margaret's voice was weak. "They were delayed by bad weather."

"Then they'll be too late, we could have visitors at any moment. We'll have to get out of here and call up the trawler."

"Out of here! Where to? What trawler?"

Larren explained as briefly as he could.

When he had finished Margaret said, "Then I'd better get on the radio and try and contact them. What's their name or call sign?"

Larren said flatly, "It isn't that easy, Doctor. You radio the trawler and you tell that Russian patrol boat exactly what's going on at the same time. They're tuned in on your wavelength remember."

"Then how — ?"

"Simple. Hidden aboard that crashed plane there's a compact device known as a homer. It emits a continuous signal that will mean nothing to the Russians even if they do pick it up. But it will bring the navy boys scurrying to collect us. All we have to do is to retrieve the homer from the plane, get to the sea, and then start it bleeping and wait."

Margaret stared at him. "Simple you

276

say! Don't you realise that there's a blizzard blowing outside?"

"I realise. But if we wait here the Russians are eventually going to walk in and round us up."

There was silence. Margaret's expression was baffled, almost unbelieving. Nina looked scared. Carver's ravaged face was grim, so was Cleyton's.

Larren said at last, "Put your furs on, Margaret, and find one of the Lapps to guide us back to the plane. See if you can get a couple to carry Carver's stretcher for us."

She said helplessly, "They won't do it — not in a blizzard."

"Ask them!" Larren's voice became harsher. "Remind them that you saved their lives during the summer when they were all sick."

"All right." She turned wearily. "I'll try." She went to get her furs.

Cleyton said grimly, "I'll go with her, Simon. There's no way of telling how close the Russians are."

Larren nodded. He was too tired to argue.

Margaret came back a few minutes later, all ready to go outside. Cleyton unslung his sten and went with her. Larren heard the outer door slam behind them and then looked down slowly, for the first time, at his left hand. The palm of his white nylon inner glove was soiled by streaks of red and he wondered how much blood he really was losing. His shirt sleeve was sticking to his arm all the way down.

A hand gripped his wrist. He had forgotten Nina Petrovitch and had not noticed her stand up from the bed. She said quietly:

"You'd better let me look at it, Simon. The bandages need tightening up."

Larren looked into the large brown eyes and forced a smile.

"There's no time, Nina. We've got to get Joe ready to travel. Besides, it's not actually bleeding now. I've kept it pretty still since we left the launch, and to move it about while getting my furs on and off will probably do more harm than good. It's best left alone until we reach the trawler."

Nina stood close to him. "Do you believe that we really will reach your trawler?"

"We'll reach it," he assured her. "There's a few tough hours ahead, but after that it will all be over." His right arm moved around her waist and he squeezed gently. "Don't worry, Nina. I forced you into this mess — but at least I'll get you out of it."

She stared up at him, her eyes still uncertain, wanting to believe but still afraid. Larren moved his right hand higher to cup the back of her neck beneath the flaring swan's tail of silk-soft hair and he kissed her full on the lips. She pressed closer, her mouth yielding and her body demanding protection. Her arms went round him almost desperately and there was as much fear as lust in her embrace. At last he allowed her mouth to slip from under his own and for a moment cradled her head on his shoulder. Then he pushed her gently away.

He had almost forgotten that Joe Carver still lay silently in his bed on the far side of the glowing stove, and now he felt a twinge of guilt. He said quietly, "We'd better find a stretcher for Joe before the others get back."

Nina smiled obediently and dropped her hands away from him. Larren gave her shoulder a final reassuring grip and then turned towards Margaret Norstadt's surgery. He remembered seeing two stretchers standing in one corner when the blonde Norwegian doctor had first shown him the dead fish that had crackled so sinisterly as it registered on the geiger counter. They were the very stretchers in which he and Carver had been carried from the plane and now he selected one of them for the return trip.

Nina was already examining Carver when Larren re-entered the hospital ward, and while she helped the stunt-man into his clothes and furs Larren gave a brief account of the events that had taken place on the Soviet island across the straits. Carver listened without comment until he had finished, and then said grimly:

"You sound as though you had a

lot of luck, Larren. Let's just hope it continues."

Larren looked at him strangely, without quite knowing why. He had the fleeting impression that there was a fine shade of hidden meaning somewhere behind Carver's tone, but he wasn't sure. Nothing showed on the scarred face and Carver's eyes were expressionless. Then Larren remembered that he had aroused the stunt-man's dislike over his rough handling of Margaret Norstadt, and he realised that perhaps he had increased that dislike by recounting how he had equally ruthlessly forced Nina Petrovitch into aiding his escape.

He decided sourly that Joe Carver might well be the best stunt-man, car, boat and plane crasher in the business, but as an espionage agent he was a wash-out. Carver was too much of a gentleman.

Then, before he had any more time to dwell upon the subject, they heard the outer door crash open. Larren automatically reached for his sten, but Adrian Cleyton knew better than to come through the second door into the hospital without identifying himself first. Larren relaxed as the slim man came back into the ward with Margaret behind him, but his moment of relaxation was short-lived.

Cleyton ripped down his face mask and said bluntly, "We've got about five minutes, Simon. That patrol boat has just arrived at the mouth of the inlet — and it looks as though they're landing a full-scale invasion."

17

Through the Blizzard

Larren's unsmiling mouth and grey-green eyes hardened in unison as he reached for his sten gun for the second time. This time he retained it in his hand.

"Where are they now, Cleyt?"

"I should imagine that they're just about coming ashore. I heard the sound of the boat's screws while Margaret was talking to the Lapps, so I followed the ice along the inlet until I reached the sea. All that I could see in that muck out there was a faint glimmer of yellow light — I guess it would have been really brilliant on an ordinary night or I wouldn't have seen it at all. By then the boat's engines had stopped and I couldn't hear anything above that infernal wind, but it was pretty obvious that they must have been using the lights to lower a boat. I doubled back along the inlet as quickly as I could."

Larren was on his feet now. "What about the Lapps?"

"They're just behind us." It was Margaret who answered.

"I've got three of them, a father and two sons. They say it is madness, but all three feel that they owe me their lives after the epidemic. Because of that they will guide us."

"Then you'd better bring them in. Joe is just about ready to travel."

Margaret looked suddenly angry as she realised that Nina had already prepared her patient, but common sense quickly washed the reaction away and she called to the three Lapp islanders. They shuffled in like a trio of shaggy brown bears in their heavy furs, their faces round and yellowish inside the deep overhang of their hoods. None of them looked very happy, and apart from the fact that their leader was grizzled and older than the other two they were identical. They looked at Margaret expectantly and waited.

Carver was all ready in his furs, and Cleyton and the two women carefully

284

transferred him to the stretcher that Larren had laid beside his bed. They swiftly stripped the ward of blankets to wrap around him and then Margaret found a waterproof fur covering to go on top. Carver bitterly cursed his incapacity once, apologised to the two women for his language in almost the same breath, and then bore the preparations in stolid silence. Three minutes later they were ready to leave.

They fitted on snow-shoes with feverish fingers, and Larren, who had had a short start while the others attended Carver, was the first one on his feet. He nodded to the two young Lapps to pick up the stretcher, and with his gloves in his pocket and the sten in his hands he led the way outside. The corridor was full of slush and when he opened the outer door it was like lifting the curtain on a black nightmare.

Larren didn't dare let himself think about it. He simply plunged outside. Cleyton followed him and they stood like sentinels on either side of the door, each staring into the raging storm in search of the Russian landing party that could be anywhere in the night. The old Lapp appeared with his two sons carrying the stretcher immediately behind him. The two women came last and both flinched bodily as they left the shelter of the medical post.

Margaret Norstadt had already told the senior Eskimo where they wanted to go, and the man struck out boldly, finding his direction more by instinct than anything else. In a matter of moments he was blotted from sight by the swirling snow and the stretcher-bearers were following him blindly into infinity. Margaret looked back once at the long wooden hut that had been her home for so long, and then hurried to walk beside the stretcher. Larren slammed the door of the hut and he and Cleyton moved to catch up. Thirty seconds later the hut was lost in snow-lashed blackness behind them, and only the vague outline of the two women remained ahead.

Cleyton moved close to Larren and shouted grimly, "Cover the rear, Simon. I'll move up to the head of the column with the old man."

Larren nodded in agreement and Cleyton lengthened his stride and forged ahead. Soon he was lost from view. Larren closed up with Nina and they kept close to the heels of the stretcher-bearers and Margaret Norstadt.

The cold was bitter and the blizzard building up to its height, and after a moment Larren slung his sten back on his shoulder and gratefully pushed his numbed hands into his gloves. The thickly driving snow was swiftly blotting out their tracks and he doubted if the Russians could find them now. What was really worrying him was whether they could find the plane. Their Lapp guide had been confident enough of his direction when he left the hut, but could he maintain it now that he had left the only landmark he could hope to recognise? Despite his assurances to Nina, Larren felt that their chances were less than slim. They could only push on and hope.

For over an hour they struggled forwards through the icy hell of the Arctic night. The winds shrieked and raged like brawling demons, slashing and scoring the frozen surface of the island wasteland. Great gusts tore through jagged ice crags and hurled themselves frenziedly across the empty snow-fields, churning the swirling maelstrom of hissing snow flakes into a devil's brew of ultimate horror. The blizzard was a clawing monster with flying cloaks of white-streaked darkness, and the winds were ghouls that screamed and lusted for frozen corpses. And above all there was the cold, the bitter, gnawing, heartfreezing cold.

Nina began to flag and Larren used his right arm to support her. He too was beginning to tire, for although his left arm had stopped throbbing and now hung stiff and useless by his side, the reaction had left him considerably weakened. He began to fear a new enemy then — exhaustion. He had believed that once they reached the plane and retrieved the vital homing transmitter they would be practically safe, for on an island, even in this weather, it should not be difficult to find the sea where the trawler could pick them up.

But now, with weariness draining every muscle, he was not so sure. Even if they reached the plane the blizzard could still bury them in exhausted heaps before they reached the sea.

The blurred outline of the Lapp Eskimo carrying the end of Carver's stretcher became almost invisible in the obscurity ahead, and Larren had to urge Nina to greater efforts to keep up. He knew that if once they fell behind the main party they were doomed, for it would be utterly hopeless to call out to the others in winds that would simply fling their voices away into the howling void. The blizzard was master here and was spiting them with terrible fury for their puny defiance.

The weight of piling snow was heavy on their shoulders now and Larren wondered how the two young Lapps were faring beneath the muscle-tearing burden of Carver's stretcher. Joe Carver was a heavy man and together with his blankets and the snow that must be building up on top the strain of carrying him must be becoming intolerable. Larren wondered then how long the Eskimoes would carry on with what to them must be madness. How much loyalty did they owe to Margaret Norstadt for saving their lives? And if they decided to give up and turn back to Stadhaven — what then?

There was no answer, and no other course of action but to push on. The blizzard had reached its height now and the more predominant winds had shifted to the east and were blasting in constant, deafening rage that all but forced them back. It was nightmarish, hellish, the end of the world beyond which nothing lived and tortured desolation reigned. It was then that Larren began to question whether the wind had really shifted round to the east, or whether their unseen guide had stumbled off course and lost his way. How could the man possibly tell where he was going in this hideous, below-zero emptiness of snow and ice? And how could be, Larren, tell whether the guide was still there? Apart from himself and Nina, and the half-seen outline of shoulders lurching ahead, there was nothing visible in the blizzard. The vague shape ahead began to remind him of Charon, the guide of damned souls who ferried them along the black waters of the Styx to the places of the dead. And it was then that he began to ask himself whether his mind was weakening as well as his body.

Nina was dragging heavily on him now, and Larren gave up hope and resigned himself to death. He had always expected to die suddenly and violently, for in the shadowy world of intrigue death was the eternal playmate. But now that death was near he told himself bitterly that it wouldn't be sudden nor violent enough. He would have preferred the swift thrust of a knife or the plunging kiss of a bullet, the killer blow from a trained hand or the fleeting sensation of his car blowing up in his face as he turned the ignition key. He would, in fact, have preferred almost anything except the slow, creeping death of lying face down on the ice while exhaustion and savage cold drained the last remnants of life from his collapsed body. Except that he wasn't going to lie down and die, he spoke the words in his mind with desperate ferocity, if he was going to die, then he would die, but at least he would go on until he froze on his feet.

His mind was so preoccupied with death that he did not realise that the blizzard was losing its murderous force, that the wind was relenting and no longer shrieked in such frenzy, or that the snow was beginning to swirl less thickly. His head was bowed low in supplication to the elements and he was following the feet of the rear Eskimo instead of his shoulders. The feet stopped suddenly and Larren almost collided with the man before he could blunder to a halt, checking Nina's progress at the same time.

He straightened his back, and with the sense of observing a miracle he found that he could distinguish all five members of the party in the gloom. Isolated flakes of snow still spun around them and the wind still ruled the glacial world, but the worst of the blizzard had abated. The two squat figures with the stretcher were silent and immobile, but Margaret

Norstadt had moved forward to confer with Cleyton and their guide.

Ten minutes later they found the plane. They had walked past it in the blizzard, but the old Eskimo knew almost exactly the distance they had walked and was confident of his own sense of direction. He led them round in a slow, careful circle and then abruptly stopped and pointed. Larren and Nina had caught up with the head of the column now, and Larren had to stare hard and long into the darkness before the snow-covered outline of the old Blenheim gradually merged into shape. It was impossible to tell whether they had missed it by ten yards or a hundred, but if the blizzard had not blown itself out in time they would have missed it altogether.

Larren moved forward with Cleyton to inspect the plane, and was surprised to find that it was still all in one piece. The tail was cocked high, and although the nose looked at first as though it must be crushed and buckled against the large hummock that had brought her erratic course to a stop, it had in fact been cushioned by a layer of soft snow and was practically undamaged. Even the propellers were still intact.

Larren moved round towards the uplifted tail and abruptly the snow ended beneath his feet and he half-slipped and half-fell on to a surface of smooth ice. He realised then why their guide had been so confident of finding the plane even in the blizzard. The Blenheim had come to rest half-way up the bank of a wide inlet that cut in deeply from the sea, the old man had only needed to strike into the solid, glacial river and then follow its course. He thought grimly that if Margaret Norstadt had only seen fit to mention that at the outset she could have spared him a lot of morbid thinking, and he wondered whether she had deliberately tried to even scores with him by letting him sweat it out — if sweat it out was the right phrase in these conditions.

He turned back to the nose of the plane and pushed that last thought out of his mind. Now that they had found the Blenheim it did not really matter. The very act of finding the plane had given him new hope, for even if they could not reach the sea a landing party from the trawler could come ashore and pick them up once they set the homing signal into operation. In the circumstances he felt that he could now tolerate any minor indications of the enmity that Doctor Margaret might still feel towards him.

The Lapps had set Carver's stretcher down in the slight wind-break created by the large hillside of drifted snow, and the two women waited beside them while Larren and Cleyton approached the plane. Larren had found new strength as well as hope in their reprieve from the blizzard, and with the help of a strong push from Cleyton he clambered up on to the starboard wing. When he straightened up he was above the level of the hill-top, and the still powerful wind almost blew him off again. He wavered clumsily, his feet slipping through five inches of snow that buried the surface of the wing, and then he regained his balance. He moved forward to the roof of the fuselage and examined the sliding hatch cover above the pilot cabin. Margaret Norstadt had thoughtfully closed the hatch behind her when they had last left the plane, and now it was frozen into place.

Larren heaved at it clumsily with his one hand, and then Cleyton pulled himself on to the wing and moved up beside him. The slim man indicated that he should wait, for the wind was still strong enough to make conversation difficult, and then he unslung his sten gun from his shoulder. Larren shifted back out of the way and Cleyton carefully removed the magazine from his sten before using the butt as a battering ram to slam at the edge of the hatch. On the third blow it moved, and after the fifth he was able to push it open.

Larren produced his torch and shone it down into the cabin. There was a smear of dried blood inside the window where his head had made contact, and the broken shoulder strap still dangled uselessly from the back of his chair, but apart from that there was no sign that the Blenheim had crashed at all. Straighten her up, Larren thought, and she might even fly again. That's if the wind ever lets up on this God-forsaken part of the Arctic.

He started to swing his legs inside the hatch but a hand stopped him. Cleyton pulled down his face mask and shouted.

"I'll get it, Simon. Just tell me where."

Larren hesitated. He had worked alone for so long that it had become a habit to rely only upon himself, but Cleyton was not hampered by one useless arm and it was childish to refuse the slim man's offer. He tugged down his own mask and shouted back.

"It's the first-aid box. Underneath the pilot's seat."

Cleyton nodded and dropped down into the cockpit. It took him less than a minute to drag the foot-square black box with its brightly-painted red cross from beneath the seat, and then he handed it up to Larren and climbed out again over the back of the seats. Larren steadied the box on the fuselage and used his good hand to help pull Cleyton out. Then together they slid down the slope of the wing to land feet first in the snow and rejoin the two women.

Both doctors looked doubtfully at the tin box as Cleyton placed it on the snow beside Carver's stretcher. Here in the combined shelter of the plane and the snow-covered hummock that had brought it to a halt it was possible to talk without the wind scattering their words before anyone else had a chance to hear them. Margaret looked at Larren and said acidly.

"Are you sure this is what you brought us out here for?"

Larren nodded. He opened the lid to reveal bandages and dressings, and all the usual contents of a standard first-aid kit. He said flatly:

"We couldn't afford to make this thing obvious, because we knew we would have to leave it on the plane and we were sure that the Russians would be nosing round the wreckage very soon after Joe and I had been carried away. But there's a three-quarter-inch false bottom on this particular first-aid box and the homing device is built into that."

He demonstrated the information by removing his outer glove and pressing the bottom of the box beneath the bandages. The whole box swung up smoothly, complete with contents, and left merely a false bottom that was built up with a complicated maze of wires and transistors.

"These can be made in miniature," Larren continued. "But that trawler is several hours north of here and we had to allow for the foulest weather conditions. We had to make sure that the signal carried enough range to be picked up." He pushed a tiny switch that clicked into place, and then closed the box up. "We hear nothing," he said. "But on the receiving screen aboard the trawler the signal has already started up like a radar blip. They'll be cutting the nets adrift now and heading for the nearest point of land. We could just sit here and wait. They've got a portable receiver that will enable them to come ashore and find us, but we'll keep warmer and save time if we start walking to the sea."

He looked up. "Margaret, you can send your friends home now. Just get them to point out the quickest way to — "

He stopped as the oldest Lapp suddenly sat up and spoke, pointing into the darkness where the wind still swirled lonely flakes of snow. Cleyton was already grabbing for his sten and Larren spun round in alarm with the homer still in his hands.

A figure in furs loomed out of the night, hurrying towards them. The old man started forward and Margaret grabbed at Cleyton's arm to stop him levelling his sten.

"It's only one of the islanders," she shouted desperately. "He's too short and stubby to be anything else."

Cleyton stopped and waited. Larren lowered the vital black box to the snow and said grimly.

"Find out what's happening."

Margaret nodded and moved forward to join the old man who was now conversing with the newcomer. The old man turned towards her and spoke swiftly, and after a few moments she came back with the two Eskimoes behind her.

"It is another one of his sons," she said

grimly. "The boy followed us through the blizzard."

Larren stared at the squat Eskimo youth who now leaned heavily on his father for support. The boy's breathing was a harsh gasping sound that even the wind couldn't drown, and erratic clouds froze in front of his face each time he exhaled. He looked completely spent and staggered slightly as they came to a stop. Larren thought of the blizzard that had just passed and found he couldn't believe it. Nobody could have followed them through that!

But the evidence was undeniable, and sudden fear shivered into his stomach.

He said harshly, "Why?"

Margaret looked at him with hatred in her fine silver-grey eyes. She said coldly:

"Because the men from the patrol boat went to the settlement when they found that we had left the medical post. They beat one of the Eskimoes until he confessed that I had asked Otuk and his two sons to guide us here to the aeroplane. Then the men ordered the beaten man to guide them here also.

The boy was afraid for his family, if they lose three strong men the whole family will starve. So he came to warn them, passing the men from the patrol boat in the storm. There are a dozen men in the Russian party, and he is afraid that they will kill his father and his older brothers for helping us." She paused, then finished, "I have already told Otuk to take his sons and go. They cannot help us any more."

Larren turned away slowly and looked down at the black box emitting its silent signal at his feet, and bitterly realised that he might just as well switch it off. With an Eskimo guide the Russians would have no difficulty in finding the plane. And although they could push on into the Arctic night there was no longer enough snow falling to smother their tracks. The Russians would catch them long before Smith's Navy-manned trawler could perform its simple rescue duty.

18

The Greatest Sacrifice

There was silence in the black Arctic night. Silence but for the grim wailing of the wind that swept over the small party huddled against the vague, snow-shrouded shape of the crashed Blenheim, but the wind was such a constant feature that it was now just another part of the freezing background of snow and ice and failed to register separately. Margaret Norstadt still faced Larren with accusing eyes as he looked up from the homing transmitter at his feet. Larren had nothing to say. Cleyton still gripped his sten and stared into the barrier of snow-flecked darkness from which they had come. The two young Lapps slowly moved away from Carver's stretcher and stood anxiously by their father and younger brother.

Then Nina said in a tense voice,

"Couldn't we split up? Perhaps one party could get away."

Cleyton answered, quietly but still loud enough for all to hear, "No, Nina. If there's a dozen men following us then they can split into two parties also. And besides, we only have the one transmitter." His voice became bitter. "If only that damned blizzard could have held off until now. With a storm to cover our tracks they would never find us once we left the plane."

"Wait a minute!" Joe Carver had pulled himself on to one elbow on his stretcher. "Nina could be right. You won't all get away, but one of you might make it. You, Cleyt. You're the fittest. You could take the homer and strike off alone.

On your own you could keep ahead and just keep moving along the coast until that trawler does get here. At least you'll get the report back to Smith — that's the main thing."

Cleyton hesitated, the idea of abandoning them clearly repugnant. And then Larren said grimly:

"Wait another minute. Joe, this aeroplane beside us is practically undamaged. With the Lapps to help we can pull her nose out of this snow hill and straighten her up on the ice of the inlet. It's smooth enough to make a runway and there's enough fresh snow on top to give the wheels a grip. At a pinch I think she'll fly."

Carver's scarred face became sardonic in the depths of his hood. He said harshly, "Sure. She'll fly. Next summer maybe, when it's daylight and the wind has stopped howling. *If* the props aren't buckled, and *if* we can unfreeze the engine. But right now, Larren, you'd never lift her off the ground. Especially with five people on board. There's too much weight."

Larren dropped on one knee beside the stretcher. "Listen, Joe. The props are all right. I've checked. And I've no intention of trying to take off with five people aboard. For what I have in mind I only need to get the engine started and get the plane in the air. It doesn't matter if I crash her straight into the sea."

305

Carver stared up at him, and when he spoke again there was no sarcasm left in his voice. He said slowly:

"She's been out here several days, but we just might be able to start the engine. But if anyone did try to fly her that's exactly what would happen — the winds would spin her straight into the sea. So exactly what do you have in mind?"

Larren said bluntly, "Fooling the Russians. If I can make them believe that we have all attempted to escape in the Blenheim and died in the attempt, then there's a strong chance that they'll call off the search. Especially if I can put her in the sea where they can't search the wreckage and check the number of bodies. I might be able to give the rest of you a reprieve."

Carver's face was devoid of expression, just a shadowed network of scars. He still spoke slowly:

"How are you going to induce the Russians to believe that we all took part in this crazy flight?"

"Simple. We all get into the plane before we send the Lapps back to

Stadhaven. When they're out of sight the rest of you scramble out again while I take off. Fool the Lapps and we fool the Russians, because Doctor Margaret will advise Otuk to tell them everything to avoid any further trouble for his family."

Carver said softly, "Four lives for the price of one. It might work. The Reds would hear the crash, and Otuk would tell them we were all in it. It just might work."

Larren said calmly, "That's all I wanted to know." He looked up at Margaret Norstadt. "I'm going to try it. Tell Otuk to get his sons on the tail of the plane and pull her out on to the — " He broke off and crumpled up with a choking gasp of agony as Joe Carver deliberately hit him across his injured arm.

Carver watched him as he crouched in the snow, doubled up and clutching the arm across his chest. Then the stunt-man massaged the edge of his gloved palm and said softly:

"That was only a tap, but it tells me what *I* want to know, Larren. It's going

307

to take the strength of two arms to pull that stick back and lift the Blenheim's nose off the ground, and you can't do it. Besides, you haven't the knowledge and experience. I'm the pilot — it's my job — and if she will fly then I'm going to be at the controls."

Larren said savagely, "Don't be a fool, Joe. You've got a broken leg, remember. Besides, this was my idea. I'm not asking you to — "

"Stop the glory-hogging, Larren. You've had all the fun so far. And I can manage with one leg this one time." He smiled faintly. "This is going to be Joe Carver's only contribution to the assignment. I made a mess of flying you in here, but at least I'll fly her out."

Margaret Norstadt said desperately, "Joe, you can't! Let Mr. — bloody — Larren kill himself if he wants to — but not you."

"Neither of you are going to kill yourselves," Cleyton said flatly. "I'm the only fit man here. And I can fly a plane. I'll take her out."

Carver shook his head. "No, Cleyt.

You've just explained why you have to stay behind — because you're the only really fit man here. Larren has at least got one angle straight, we need to get rid of one of the cripples. And crashing things *is* my job. That's my part in the organisation. That's what I'm paid for. Other men do the actual jobs — I create the big bangs and the diversions." The faint smile appeared again. "And another thing. My face finished a lot of things for me a long time ago, and now this leg has finished me as a stunt-jockey. I don't have to be told that it's too weak to stand any more rough stuff. So don't try and deny me my last big and glorious smash."

There was silence, and then Nina said quietly:

"He is right. He is the pilot, and if it is necessary then obviously he must fly the plane."

"Thank you," Carver smiled again. Then he looked up at Margaret Norstadt. "Tell Otuk, Margaret. Larren and Cleyt will give them a hand. The Russians must be getting close and we haven't much time."

Margaret looked back into his eyes without speaking, then she turned to face Larren and the hatred in her eyes was murderous. She started to speak, faltered, and then left the words unsaid. Larren felt unclean beneath her gaze and then she turned away and gave the necessary instructions to Otuk.

Larren and Cleyton moved to help the Lapps and Nina came with them. She said quietly:

"Leave them together, Simon. The Norwegian doctor has become very fond of your friend Carver."

Larren nodded, and felt strangely grateful for Nina's tact.

The task of getting the old fighter-bomber facing the right direction along the glacial surface of the inlet was harder than Larren had realised. Getting her nose out of the drift proved easy enough, for Cleyton and the two young Lapps simply climbed on to the roof of the fuselage and inched forwards until they reached the tail where their weight pushed it down until Larren and Otuk could get a grip from below. The tail then sank smoothly down until the tail wheel rested on the ice. But swinging the Blenheim in a half circle was a different task altogether, and the combined forces of all seven of them failed to shift the front wheels from the deep snow on the bank of the inlet. The gale-force winds taunted their efforts and swept the loosened snow from the Blenheim's wings into their faces. Larren was almost sobbing as he strained his good shoulder underneath the plane's nose and at any moment he expected the landing party from the Russian patrol boat to appear with a chorus of shouts and blazing sten guns from the swirling darkness.

Then Cleyton said desperately, "Let's try rocking her. Nina can pull on one wing. I'll take the other."

Larren nodded and waited while they moved into position. Cleyton heaved on the starboard wing and the plane swayed to the right, Nina answered with an equally violent pull from the opposite side and a miniature avalanche of sliding snow spilled off the flat surface of the wings and half-buried all of them. Larren yelled at them to keep on and while the Blenheim was rocked from side to side he and the Lapps threw their backs into another muscle-bursting thrust. The Blenheim shifted backwards, and from then on backed a matter of inches with each effort until she rolled down on to the snow-blanketed ice. Then, with Cleyton and two of the Lapps dragging on one wing, and the rest of them pushing at the other, they slowly brought the Blenheim's nose round to face into the wind.

There was no time to waste and they hurriedly returned to Carver. Margaret Norstadt stood up slowly as they approached and Larren knew from her expression that she was praying that the plane's engine would be too cold to start. But she made no more protest as Carver was carried over to the plane.

The Lapps man-handled the stretcher up on to the wing and then Cleyton and the two women took over. Margaret dropped inside the cabin to guide Carver's legs, while Cleyton and Nina helped him lower himself through the roof-top hatch. Larren could only stand by with the Lapps feeling bitterly useless.

As soon as Carver had dropped out of sight Cleyton scrambled down on to the ice again. The wind was buffeting noisily against the flanks of the Blenheim and he had to shout to make Larren hear.

"Get aboard, Simon. I'll handle the props."

Larren nodded in answer and pulled himself up on to the wing. The slim man waited with his gloved hands up-stretched to grip the propeller and awaiting Carver's signal from inside the cabin. Through the glass Larren could see Margaret helping the pilot to strap himself in. Carver gave her a final nod and then she climbed out on to the fuselage again. She pushed past Larren and jumped down to make her parting speech to their Lapp helpers. Carver raised a thumb in signal and Cleyton spun the propeller.

Larren knelt by the open roof hatch, dropped his gloves inside and unslung his sten gun as the engine spluttered. The sound of the engines was going to act like a magnet in the night, and if the pursuing Russians were closer than they

313

hoped the sten was going to be needed.

Cleyton pulled on the prop a second time, and then a third, but still the cold engine only spluttered. The Lapps had backed away and Margaret hurried back to the plane. Larren would have offered her his hand to help her on to the wing, but he knew that she would have ignored it. She didn't look at him as she dropped down through the hatch into the seat beside Carver. Nina was somewhere in the back.

Six times Cleyton spun the propeller as Carver clenched his teeth and pulled at the switches, and then on the sixth desperate swing the engine roared and the slim man staggered back as the propeller coughed, jerked, jerked again and finally became a spinning blurr.

Carver smiled, the cabin light was on and he had pushed back the hood of his parka, and the full smile made a fiendish picture of the pilot's scarred face. He nodded to Cleyton and then gestured to the opposite wing, but the slim man was already stumbling towards the second prop.

Larren's muscles tightened with the roaring of the first engine and his numbed hands froze even closer to the sten. He prayed that the second engine would start as quickly, or even faster, for the sound must now be drawing every Russian on Dog Island directly towards them at a frantic run.

Cleyton was aware of the same fact for he was spinning the second propeller with feverish urgency. Carver's savaged face had set fast into its hideous grin and his gloved hands moved the switches firmly in tune with Cleyton's effort. Larren forced his gaze away from the plane and concentrated on the windswept darkness beyond. He counted the spluttering swings on the propeller as he stared into frozen black nothingness, and after a dozen attempts the stubborn motor still refused to roar. Larren was ready to believe that the engine must have completely iced up, and then on the thirteenth swing the propeller made the same coughing, jerking motions as its sister had done. Cleyton tried again and this time there was an answering roar as the two engines blended together.

Cleyton lurched to one side, hesitated a moment and then ducked underneath the wing to climb up by the fuselage. Larren was already slithering inside the cockpit with his sten slung back over his shoulder and the slim man was only seconds behind him. Without hesitation Carver released the brakes and the Blenheim started to taxi forward with the roof hatch still open. The four squat figures of the Lapps stood and watched as they started along the frozen surface of the inlet, and then they were lost to sight.

The props roared lustily above the shriek of the wind and the plane bumped and shook as she continued to taxi through the night. Carver's face was grey and his mouth shut tight against the pain of sitting upright with his broken leg and Margaret Norstadt was equally pale beside him. Then Carver looked back and said calmly:

"We're out of sight of the Eskimoes, and clear of our starting point. You can all start abandoning ship while I taxi slowly." He smiled faintly at Larren.

"And don't worry — a Joe Carver crash is always top quality. It's my only claim to fame and I'll make it good."

Larren faltered, but there was no answer. How could he say good luck to a man about to stage his own death? There was nothing to do but grip the man's shoulder in a parting gesture and then turn away. Cleyton gave him a push as he climbed out of the hatch and the wind tore at his body as he pulled himself out on to the wing of the moving plane.

He waited until Nina joined him and together they jumped. Both of them landed feet first in the soft snow covering the ice and skidded flat on their backs as the tail-plane swished towards them. Larren rolled and his injured arm screamed with agony as the Blenheim roared past. The tail-plane missed them by inches.

The old fighter-bomber vanished snarling in the darkness, and a few minutes later they heard her engines roar even louder as she picked up speed. They knew then that Cleyton and Margaret had also jumped and that the crippled stuntman was flying alone. The wind howled in sudden, surprised fury, as if rising up in startled anger at this unexpected defiance, and then the sound of the engines began to lift and Larren knew that the Blenheim must be airborne.

* * *

Carver was again grinning fiendishly as he pulled back the stick. His large body was pushed back into the seat as he braced himself and blinding pain gushed up from his left leg like blazing oil spurting from the released pressure of a sudden strike. The white-hot flood hit his hip and the whole leg melted into tortured fire. He pulled and the Blenheim's nose lifted, bounced, lifted again and then became airborne, only to flip fifty yards and then crash down again as the winds slapped her back to earth. Carver's whole body screamed and screamed again, but no sound issued from his throat and the inhuman grin stayed frozen to his scarred face.

The Blenheim's tail was whipping frenziedly from side to side as she skimmed at full speed along the ice like some helplessly baffled bird with clipped wings. The winds used her like a paper toy as she bumped and hopped in great erratic leaps. Carver's arms knotted and his body screamed again as he leaned back in his seat, and for the second time the plane's nose lifted into the black, raging night.

Carver held her there, his face a contorted mask of ravaged flesh tissue, and for a few moments he was successful, thrusting her a hundred feet into the sky. And then the wind slammed her down again and this time there were drifting ice floes below. The Blenheim hit flat on her belly, her wheels plunging into an open channel but her nose and tail bridging solid ice with a sickening crunch that made a thousand-pound bomb sound like a fizzling flop. Both ice floes reared high in the air as the plane spun round, her back cleanly broken and the starboard wing tearing away with a shattering cracking sound as she slewed into a boiling waterspout of sea and broken ice. The towering floe looming above the cockpit stood completely upright, and then turned the full circle. The monstrous frozen tombstone of ice toppled slowly forwards, crushing the mangled wreckage and pushing it deep below the surface. The whole thunderous, tearing impact was sweet music to Carver's ears, and as the freezing black sea swirled around him his horrific grin burst into a mixed shriek of pain and triumph.

He knew that the crash had been a good one, his spectacular best, and it really did have Joe Carver's name on it.

19

Duel on the Ice

Simon Larren stood in silence as the last echoes of the crash faded into the night, and he knew that this time the Blenheim's end was final. The racing winds that still tore their violent path across the surface of Dog moaned a banshee's requiem for Joe Carver, and Larren prayed that the Lapp Otuk would not fail them in convincing the pursuing Russians that they had all been aboard the doomed plane. He knew that Margaret Norstadt would never forgive him for suggesting the ruse that had cost Carver's life, but if the attempt failed then it would be even harder to forgive himself. Then Nina pulled gently at his arm to remind him of her presence, and he realised that he could not stand for ever with his conscience in the Arctic night. It was time they found their companions.

They followed the wheel marks of the Blenheim for a hundred yards along the inlet before the bulky, fur-muffled figures of Cleyton and Margaret loomed out of the darkness a few feet ahead. Cleyton held the doctor's arm and in his free hand he carried the vital transmitter they needed to rendezvous with the navy-manned trawler. They had little to say in this moment, but Larren felt a surge of relief as he checked the transmitter and found it to be still emitting its silent signal. The one reason why he had entrusted the homer to Cleyton was because the slim man had two good arms with which to cradle it as he jumped from the moving plane.

They conferred briefly, and then continued to follow the inlet and the wheel marks towards the sea, moving in pairs with Margaret and Cleyton leading the way. They did not hurry for they had at least three to four hours before the trawler could reach them and there was no need to push themselves any further. The powerful winds were still deep below zero and made heavy going, but they concentrated upon exerting themselves just sufficiently to combat the vicious cold without tiring themselves any nearer to the point of exhaustion.

The possibility of the landing party from the Russian patrol boat being still behind them became irrelevant, for if the Russians were continuing the pursuit then they had only to follow the wheel tracks of the plane and then pick up the trail of the fugitives in the soft snow. The chase would be over long before the approaching trawler reached Dog, and so escape or capture depended entirely on whether or not the search had been called off after Carver had staged his spectacular crash. Either way speed would not help them.

However, they had little strength to conserve. Nina soon began to weaken and relied heavily upon Larren's support. Larren, too, neared the last of his brief revival. Only Cleyton appeared to have any further reserves and he in turn was having to assist Margaret Norstadt. They were all in bad shape.

Then they received an unexpected

blessing, for the darkness began to fade into a grey dawn. The psychological advantage of even the brief period of semi-daylight gave them new heart and kept them going until they reached the coast.

For a moment all four stared out across the glacial jungle of sea ice, the pattern of their thoughts linked as they searched for some sign of the crashed Blenheim. There was nothing to be seen, and Nina finally broke the respectful silence.

"Thank God we are here. Now — now perhaps we can find somewhere out of this terrible wind where we can rest."

Larren tightened his arm about her waist, and answered:

"There is nowhere out of the wind, Nina. It's all too flat. So I'm afraid we can't rest. We must keep moving slowly, just enough to keep our blood circulating and prevent ourselves from freezing. We'll keep to the coast and head north to meet the trawler as it comes down the straits. The ground we cover won't make any difference to the time we have to wait, but we have to keep moving to stay alive."

"Not north, Simon. South!" Cleyton's breathing was heavy but his voice was firm. "I can't be positive of my direction up here, but when old Otuk led us away from the medical post he was leading us roughly parallel to the path we made when coming from the launch. I think he veered a little bit north, but by turning more to the right to follow the inlet after we found the plane we must have swung back again to our original route. Consequently the launch must be somewhere down the coast to our right still, and if we must walk to stay alive then we might as well attempt to find it and the shelter it will provide. It's better than walking aimlessly, and as you've just said, the amount of ground that we cover won't really make any difference whichever direction we follow."

Larren forced himself to think clearly, examining the idea for a few minutes, and then said slowly, "You're probably right, and now that it's daylight — or at least, half-light — we should stand a good chance of finding the launch again by following the coast. But we're not sure whether that patrol boat dropped an initial landing party there before circling round to Stadhaven, and if there was a party dropped then we could walk right into them by attempting to return to the launch."

"They could have dropped a party there," Cleyton admitted. "But I doubt very much whether they would have wasted the time. They knew that the only place we could make for was the medical post and it's more likely that they headed straight for Stadhaven. But even if they did waste the time then the initial landing party would have chased after us to the settlement and is probably back at the patrol boat by now." He paused for a moment and then declared bluntly, "Let's face facts, Simon. At the earliest we can't expect that trawler before another two or three hours, and it could be much longer. In the meantime we need some kind of shelter to survive, and the cabin of that launch is the only shelter we can hope to find. The women are both at the limit of their resources, they can't keep on walking endlessly until the trawler arrives."

He could have added, "and neither can you", and although he tactfully refrained, Larren knew that he would have been equally right.

"All right, Cleyt," he said at last. "We'll move south and try to locate the launch. Either way we're gambling, but even though I don't like it we're in no position to be choosey."

Cleyton nodded and readjusted his face mask. The bitter cold was numbing their cheeks and Larren and Nina were glad to do the same. The decision was settled and there was no more to be said as they started down the white coastline. Larren could have added a warning to walk warily just in case they were wrong in expecting to find the launch unguarded, but Cleyton's training had been as thorough as his own and the words would have been a wasted insult. They were both fully alert as they searched among the cracked channels of clear water splitting into the ice field from the sea.

After half an hour Larren realised that Cleyton was undoubtedly right and that they did need to find the shelter of the launch, for Nina was staggering so badly that it was obvious that she could not keep on going for much longer. Margaret too was showing clearer signs of their strength-sapping ordeal through the blizzard and was leaning almost as heavily upon Cleyton as Nina leaned upon Larren.

Quite suddenly the once-dubious suggestion that they should attempt to find the launch became a vital necessity. He knew that Cleyton would still be alive when the trawler found them, and so, possibly, would Margaret Norstadt and himself, even though they most likely would have collapsed. But Nina had weakened too soon, if they did not find some kind of shelter to get her out of the bitter winds then Nina Petrovitch would freeze to death.

He concentrated more desperately on the search, but there was nothing but the shifting ice floes and the straits beyond. The Soviet island of Barren was again hidden in distant mist. Larren's eyes ached and he calculated that they must have travelled almost a mile down the coast, and then he began to despair. Cleyton's senses of distance and direction must have been thrown hopelessly out of balance by the blizzard and Larren was suddenly sure that they would never find the launch. Perhaps it was much further south, or perhaps they had crossed their original route somewhere in the storm and they should have been searching north, or perhaps the Russians had already retrieved it. The last thought was original, but quite possible, and hit him like a club between the eyes. Then Cleyton suddenly stopped him and pointed with the hand holding the black box of the homing transmitter, and for the first time since Larren had released him from his cell on Barren the slim man's eyes were smiling.

"Over there, Simon. See it?"

The words were muffled by Cleyton's face mask, but Larren saw it; despite the blanket of white snow that helped to camouflage it against the background of ice the outline was undoubtedly that of their launch. He stared towards it and felt a thousand years younger, and beneath his face mask he too could form a smile. The launch was jammed into the open channel of sea water exactly as they had left it, and there was no sign of life either aboard or near her.

Larren gave Nina a gentle shake that caused her to raise her head, and then indicated the boat with a stiff gesture of his left hand. She stared, and he felt her body go limp, as though relief had drained the last of her strength, and then he tightened his arm around her and pulled her unresisting across the last fifty yards of snow-covered ice. Cleyton and Margaret moved with them and all four approached together in a line abreast. When they were still thirty yards away a figure suddenly appeared on the launch's deck.

The man was unmistakably a Russian, for none of the Lapp islanders carried anything so modern as a sten gun slung across their backs. For a fraction of a second he too was shocked by surprise, and then he grabbed at the gun.

Adrian Cleyton was momentarily hamstrung by the homing transmitter in his hand and the fact that Margaret was hanging on to his waist. But Larren had been wholly supporting Nina and when he thrust her away she simply sprawled on to the snow. He ran for the launch with frantic, shuffling strides in his awkward snow-shoes, stripping off his gloves as he ran and throwing them into the snow.

The man on the launch had made the fatal mistake of unslinging his sten while his hands were still encumbered by his thick gloves. He fumbled to fire, failed, and then turned to run as he saw Larren levelling his own sten with free hands. Larren fired but his fingers were numbed solid and the clumsy burst missed its target and ripped splinters of flying ice and woodwork off the roof of the launch's cabin.

The bulky figure in furs had already scrambled out of the launch and was zig-zagging desperately across the ice on the far side of the channel. He was crouching low as he fumbled to discard his gloves and for the moment the raised superstructure of the launch was blocking Larren from another clear shot. Behind them Cleyton had disentangled himself from Margaret Norstadt and was sprinting in pursuit.

Larren crossed the cracked channel in the ice in two strides, using the stern of the launch as a stepping stone. His foot slipped in the snow on the smooth woodwork and he all but skidded to a freezing death in the black water before tumbling down on to his knees on the far edge of the ice. The man from the launch had succeeded in shedding his gloves and had stopped twenty yards away to turn and face him. Both sten guns erupted into a stuttering bark in the same moment.

Snow and ice sprayed up in a ricocheting curtain six feet in front of Larren's face, and through it he saw his opponent spinning round like a whipped top, the chattering sten in his hands still throwing bullets in an aimless arc through the sky.

Instinct had caused Larren to jerk his

head and shoulders back as the spray flew up in front of him, and even as he watched the other man fall he felt himself slipping backwards over the edge of the ice. He dropped his sten frantically and twisted to save himself, hooking his right arm over the stern of the launch. His feet scrambled helplessly as they slithered to the edge of the ice and another second would have immersed him totally in the icy waters.

Cleyton reached the launch in time to see the lone Russian topple over in a sprawling, fur-covered heap, and automatically he kicked open the cabin door to check inside. The launch was empty, and satisfied that there was no more danger he looked for Larren. He saw the one arm hanging on to the stern of the launch and the snow-shoes now balanced on the very edge of the ice and made the fastest move of his life. Larren's outer furs had already dipped into the bitter Arctic sea as the slim man hauled him out.

For several minutes Larren was incapable of standing without Cleyton's help. The unexpected burst of action had once more woken the dormant agony of his left arm and his legs were trembling weakly.

Cleyton said grimly, "You'd better get inside the cabin, Simon. I'll go back for the women and the transmitter."

Larren forced himself to stand alone and looked back to Margaret and Nina who both lay where they had fallen on the ice. Then he turned his gaze to the other side of the channel towards the man he had shot.

He said slowly, "Perhaps we'd better take a look at him first. There might be enough life left in him to fire that sten again."

Cleyton hesitated, then nodded. "It's possible. And I'd hate to be shot in the back by a dying effort."

They climbed out of the launch and Larren paused to pick up his sten before they cautiously approached the still figure. The wind was, as always, the dominant feature of the polar landscape, and Larren wondered whether it really was merely his imagination that made it sound like the wailing of a banshee every time there was the scent of death over the ice.

The man was completely motionless and Cleyton kicked the fallen sten gun away from his outstretched hand. Larren knelt over the body and laid his own gun to one side as he pulled down the face mask and goggles. The movement revealed a square, strangely American-type face with short, brush-cut hair. Larren stared in complete astonishment.

Cleyton said slowly, "It's Kerensky. But what — ?" He stopped and stared down at the man in baffled silence. Larren finished what the slim man had been about to say, his voice soft but gradually becoming harsh.

"But what is Barren Island's chief of security police doing out here alone? Retrieving, or standing guard over the launch, isn't the kind of job he'd do himself. And if he suspected that Carver took off in the plane alone and that we might attempt to use the launch again, then why is he on his own and not with the rest of the landing party from the patrol boat?"

Cleyton had recovered his composure.

"I don't know," he said grimly. "But somewhere, something stinks."

It was then that Kerensky's eyelids flickered, and they realised that there was still a fading spark of life in his crumpled body. His eyes opened fully and he looked up at them, recognition glittered, and the hard corners of his mouth showed the faint traces of a smile.

Cleyton knelt closer so that the security major could hear him above the noise of the wind. He spaced his questions carefully and insistently so that the man could not fail to understand.

"Why are you out here, Kerensky? Why are you alone? And what were you looking for on the launch?"

Kerensky's smile became stronger and he answered feebly, but deliberately in Russian. He spoke just one sentence and then looked past Cleyton's shoulder and finished in English.

"You too, Mr. Larren. You are *another* bloody fool!"

And then he closed his eyes and died. For a moment there was silence but for the taunting of the wind, and then both Larren and Cleyton looked up from the dead man's face and stared at each other. Then Larren spoke slowly, as though reciting a lesson that was still not quite clear.

"He spoke to you in Russian. But it wasn't a mental slip because he reverted to English to speak to me."

"Which means," Cleyton said tightly, "that I wasn't fooling them at all. And if he knew all along that I speak Russian, then everything that I overheard was false information that I was meant to overhear."

As he spoke they both sensed the almost silent movement on the ice behind them, and the same thought struck them simultaneously. They both whirled to face the fur-muffled figure that had approached behind them and Larren had hurled himself half-way towards her before he could stop himself.

Nina Petrovitch pointed the Russian automatic in her hand at his face and rasped harshly:

"You are perfectly right. We knew from

the start that Cleyton understands the Russian language. There is a fat dossier containing his record in the files of the K.G.B. headquarters in Moscow. And one for you too — clever, Mr. Simon Larren."

20

The Secret of Barren Island

Under the threat of the automatic Larren sank slowly back on to one knee on the ice. He stared at the bitter hatred mirrored in Nina's eyes and still could not quite bring himself to believe it. His sten gun still lay by Kerensky's body only a yard away, but in that moment it might as well have been on the other side of the Arctic. Cleyton had already re-slung his sten across his shoulder and it would have been equally suicidal for him to attempt to bring it back down. Neither of them dared to move.

Then Larren found his voice and said slowly, "You fooled us beautifully, Nina. But why? And where did you get the gun?"

Nina said flatly, "The gun was all ready in the pocket of my parka. I knew exactly which set of furs to take when we passed through the guardroom on Barren."

"I see. And everything that Cleyt overheard — everything that you told me — it *was* all a blind."

"Not exactly." The large, once-tender brown eyes were now cold and almost glazed, but her tone still had the same flat, controlled note. "Barren Island *is* the central point for our undersea test range. The technicians there *are* working on extending the range of deep level communications between submarines. And they *are* investigating new aspects of sub-marine warfare. And the base is *also* a combined listening post for a highly sensitive seismograph measuring the earth disturbances of western nuclear tests from beneath the sea."

She paused there and smiled unpleasantly. "In fact, Larren, everything that I told you, and everything that Cleyton was allowed to hear was all perfectly true. And we were prepared to let the West know all about it. After all it is only details and findings that must be kept secret, for it is practically impossible to hush up the fact that these broad lines of research are taking place. Months ago when the British and American defence chiefs were discussing the plans for your own operation AUTEC the meetings were reported quite openly in your newspapers."

She smiled again, bitterly. "Of course, we could not simply report our plans in *Pravda* in the same way, it would have been completely out of character for us to explain things to the mass of peasants. But when you two blundering fools appeared we decided to simply allow you to escape with the information — information that other western agents in other spheres must have eventually uncovered in time, but which in the meantime would satisfy your intelligence forces and decrease the risk of any concentrated attention on Barren Island."

"So there's something else on Barren," Cleyton spoke softly. "Something apart from the research station that really is top secret."

"And we were allowed to escape." The stressed word brought a sour taste to Larren's mouth. "Once or twice I had the feeling that we were just a little too lucky. Finding you alone in the surgery, and then finding the launch so conveniently empty at the jetty, they both seemed almost too good to be true. But while it was happening there was no time to waste in being doubtful."

Nina's mouth shook with contemptuous laughter. "So you thought you were being lucky," she said. "You poor fool. We were falling over ourselves in order to help you. We intended at first that I should help Cleyton to escape, after we had allowed him to overhear more solid proof of my supposed fear and hatred towards Kerensky. We were undecided whether Kerensky should rape me, or whether he should simply beat me and threaten me with arrest for some feigned security charge unless I promised to sleep with him. Either way it would have been staged while Cleyton was waiting in my surgery for a medical check, and afterwards I would have begged him to find me asylum in England in return for helping him. But you saved us all the bother, Larren. You rushed things and we simply gave you your head. There was less chance of either of you suspecting the truth that way."

"Please go on," Larren's voice was still sour. "Tell us all."

"And why not?" she returned coldly. "It is too late to stop. And it pleases me to explain how foolish you have been. You may remember the illiterate soldier who was always on duty in my surgery. That was Lieutenant Malik, Kerensky's aide. He speaks English perfectly, understood everything that was going on, and watched every move you made in stealing that scalpel from my desk. You may remember also searching your cell for a camera peephole. You did not find one, but there was one there, in both your cells. Not in the ceiling or in the walls which you searched so thoroughly, but in the floor, set at a slight angle that enabled us to cover most of the room." She laughed suddenly. "The camera had an infra-red lens that enabled us to watch you in the dark, we saw you in Cleyton's cell passing handsy-pansy messages like two of your Piccadilly fairies. It was very funny."

Neither man laughed, but the gun in her hand stayed perfectly steady and neither dared move from their half-kneeling, half-crouching positions by Kerensky's body. Nina smiled at them and went on.

"When you went back to your cell, Larren, we watched you playing with that stolen scalpel. We thought that you intended to use it to murder your guards, but that would have been all right for we had deliberately supplied you with the most stupid guards available and they were quite expendable. Although I must admit that we almost rushed to stop you when you put the scalpel to your own throat, the last thing we wanted was for you to commit suicide.

"However, we watched every move you made as you released Cleyton. There were hidden cameras along the corridor as well as inside the cells and the whole performance was quite fascinating in a brutal sort of way. I was so entranced that I almost failed to get back to my office so that you could find me so conveniently. We guessed that you would need a guide and come looking for me. I played my semi-reluctant part out as long as I could to give Kerensky time to get the launch into place at the jetty."

"And to warn the men at the guardroom I suppose."

She shook her head. "No, Larren. The men in the guardroom were not warned. We credited you with being capable of tackling those without help, and although we wanted you to escape we did not want to make it easy enough for you to become suspicious. That was why Kerensky kept up the pressure all the way, first with the patrol boat and then the landing party here on this island. We had to make your escape as difficult and harassed as possible, but we still had to be sure that at least one of you did get away. It was a very delicate operation."

There was silence but for the tearing progress of the winds. Larren searched beyond Nina's menacing form but there was no hope of any reprieve. The spot where Margaret Norstadt had collapsed

345

in the snow was hidden by the launch, but although Nina had been faking it was obvious that Margaret had not. And even if the blonde Norwegian doctor did revive slightly there would be nothing that she could do. Nina was too tensely alert to allow anyone to cross the ice behind her as he and Cleyton had unsuspectingly done.

Then Cleyton said grimly, "So you staged all that phoney hatred with Kerensky, and you would even have allowed him to rape you for the sake of fooling me." His voice became distasteful. "You must be really fond of the Communist Party."

At that she laughed, almost hysterically. "You fools — you still do not understand. It would have meant nothing if Kerensky had raped me. I would have enjoyed it, as I have enjoyed it a thousand times before." Her voice pitched to a scream. "Stefan Kerensky was my husband."

She was trembling with both tears and rage and neither of them dared speak again until her hand steadied around the gun. Larren was numb with cold but still

346

the sweat of fear was forming along his spine. Then Cleyton said almost gently:

"I suppose there was some arrangement for you to be kidnapped and returned to him after you had been granted British asylum."

She nodded. "It would only have meant a separation of a few months, and it would have brought quick promotion to Stefan. The only part that was really repugnant lay in making up to Larren in order to convince you both that I really was on your side."

Larren choked on his pride, swallowed it bitterly, and then demanded, "But why did Kerensky ruin everything that he himself had planned by coming here? But for this we would never have realised that we had been duped, and within a matter of hours we would have been heading back for England with exactly the report he wanted us to make. So why was he here?"

Nina looked at him with anguish in her eyes. "Because he loved me. Can't you see that. *I was his wife*. When the plane crashed he must have believed

347

that we were all dead as you planned. But he wouldn't want to believe it. He would have prayed that it wasn't so. He undoubtedly called off the search, but for himself he had to be sure. It was wrong of him — weak of him — but for his own peace of mind he must have needed definite evidence that I was either alive or dead. No doubt he realised that if any of us still lived there was a chance that we would return to the launch. Perhaps he meant to search the whole of this coastline for any wreckage or bodies from the plane, and simply looked into the boat in the vague hope that I might have left him a message there somehow. How can I know what he thought? I can only know that the only reason for Stefan to be here was because he loved me."

Larren was silent, understanding. There was no way of knowing what desperate hopes had been in Kerensky's mind as he searched for the woman he feared was dead. The only certain thing, as Nina had said, was that he was here because he loved her. Blind fate had caused their paths to cross, or perhaps it was not fate but simply the banshees wailing in the wind, forcing them together in the craving lust for death. And now Kerensky lay beside them, and Nina still held the levelled automatic.

She went on harshly, "I knew it had to be Stefan as soon as the shooting started, but I was too late to do anything about it. But I can — and will — amend that now. You are both going to die for the murder of my husband, but first there is more salt to rub in your wounds. First you can know how the whole capitalist world will die!"

Cleyton said quietly, "You mean that you will tell us the real secret of Barren Island. The secret behind the secret that we were to have carried home."

"Exactly. The secret behind the secret." Nina inched back slightly to lengthen the distance between them, making absolutely sure that they would have no chance to jump at her once she had finished talking. She raised her voice above the wind.

"I don't know how much you know about the subject of radio technology, or what is known generally as Radio

Frequency Interference. But the term RFI covers the effects of electro-magnetic impulses, man-made or natural, that can interrupt radio communications and foul up radar and television screens. These impulses can be generated by anything either electrical or electronic, from a vacuum cleaner jamming up your wireless to a misguided frequency wave from a space satellite triggering off its own self-destruction mechanism. Or they can be generated by lightning bolts, magnetic storms, or solar flares out in space.

"Most of these RFI impulses are natural, accidental and uncontrolled. But they have been responsible for ruining rocket launchings, space experiments, and in some cases have been indirectly suspected of causing some of the major, unexplained air disasters by interfering with the pilots' instruments. A great deal of money has been spent on both sides of the world, east and west, to rid the radio waves of these invisible impulses, but a great deal more has been spent on efforts to simulate or control them. In the latter task the scientists and radio technologists on Barren have succeeded."

Larren said slowly, "You mean that the scientists on Barren can actually create electronic impulses to make a complete mess of western communications and radar screens in the event of war?"

Nina's laughter was a peal of contempt. "Still you are too stupid to understand. We do not intend to *wait* for the event of war. To wait would give the British and the Americans the necessary time to equal our achievements. You asked me once, Larren, why we chose this particular spot in the Arctic, so close to western Norway. I do not remember what ridiculous tale I told you, but the real reason is because this island is exactly opposite to a similar island in the Bering strait across the top of the polar ice cap. Each base houses a device capable of throwing thousands of these controlled electronic impulses above the ice cap, and the collision when these two beams of frequency waves meet will create panic along the great chain of radar bowls that the Americans have installed across Greenland and the Canadian Arctic. We can fill those radar screens with enough magnetic blips to convince them that the mightiest missile and bomber flight the world has ever seen is howling towards them."

Larren stared at her in silence, and was suddenly convinced that she was mad. But when he spoke his voice was still thick with nameless fear. "Even if your people can do this," he said feebly, "what good will it do them? They will only call the western bomber and missile fleets down upon their own necks. They might just as simply launch a real attacking force as to feign one on the Distant Early Warning screens."

"Still you are too stupid to understand!" She sounded fanatical with anger. "Of course the western fleets will come, they will launch everything, but before they can reach the point of no recall, the point where rockets cannot be safely destroyed in mid-flight, the machines on Barren and in the Bering Strait will be switched off. The nuclear bombers of the west will return to their bases. And then perhaps the next day our simulated attack will be switched on again; again the western fleets will be hurriedly launched, again the RFI waves will be switched off and again the fleets will be recalled. The process will be repeated until every defence chief and bomber pilot in the West becomes a bundle of shattered nerves, and their hopeless faith in the DEW line warning system is reduced to nothing. Then the real Soviet assault can begin."

Nina smiled viciously at the two crouching men who stared up into her face and finished softly, "— now you can die for murdering my Stefan."

She fired as Larren hurled himself towards her with the desperation of a man determined not to die without a fight. He saw her fist jerk with the recoil of the automatic as the bullet slammed into his body and the banshees laughed for another death as he spun down on to the ice and cold and darkness flooded on top of him.

21

The Intuition of a Dead Man

Death was a pleasant sensation. Death was soft and deep and painless, and above all warm. The numbing cold was gone and the freezing winds no longer howled. The banshees were silent. Larren floated in the drowsy warmth, savouring the quiet peace and allowing his mind to slowly waken. It seemed incredible that he had ever feared death, when death was such a comfortable relaxation. The only thing akin to the death he had imagined was the darkness, and he had never been afraid of the dark. The night had always been his ally and friend. Then abruptly his heaven started to drop away beneath him and he opened his eyes.

It was a shock, and almost a disappointment to find that he was alive. His heaven continued to fall wildly but after a second started to

354

lift again. He was lying in the low bunk of a ship's cabin beneath the weight of half-a-dozen thick blankets. A single light swayed from the deck-head above him, and a set of yellow oilskins scraped softly back and forth inside the cabin door. A woman wearing a bright red-and-orange roll-necked sweater and dark slacks sat on a chair facing him. She leaned forward as his eyes opened, and even if he had not recognised the clothes and the smooth, yellow-blonde hair, the magnificent silver-grey eyes would have been unmistakable even in his dazed condition.

"Don't move, Larren," she ordered quietly. "I had to dig a thirty-five calibre bullet out of your right side below the ribs and it will be easier if you keep still. I'm not sure whether your Russian girl friend allowed her trigger finger to get too numbed by the cold before she decided to shoot you, or whether my shot hit her in time to deflect her aim. Either way she missed your middle by about three inches, and despite making a nasty hole she failed to puncture anything vital. You've been unconscious for over nine hours, but now that you've come out of it I think you'll live."

Larren said weakly, "You had a gun?" and was surprised at how faint and croaking his voice sounded.

She nodded, "I had Joe Carver's gun. He gave it to me while the rest of you were struggling to pull the plane out of that snowdrift. He warned me to watch Nina Petrovitch because he didn't trust her. He didn't warn you because he was certain that you wouldn't believe him, and Cleyton was too much of an unknown quality. The only person Joe felt that he could trust was me." There was pain in her eyes for a moment and then she went on, "I almost failed him. I was so numbed and tired when Cleyton dropped me to follow you that I just laid there and waited for him to come back, and it was a long time before I realised that something was wrong. That was when I managed to open my eyes and saw that Nina had vanished as well. I remembered what Joe had told me — how he had trusted me — and I just couldn't lay there and know that if I failed him then Joe would have died in vain."

She was silent, and there was nothing but the creaking of the ship as she strained in the seas, and the continual slow swish of the oilskins on the door. Then Margaret blinked to clear the moisture from her eyes and went on:

"I managed to get up and walk towards the launch. That was when I saw Nina pointing her gun at you and Cleyton. So I hid behind the launch's cabin and took out the gun that Joe had given me. I remembered everything Joe told me — I took off my gloves, and used both hands to hold the gun so that it stayed perfectly steady. And then I rested both arms on the roof of the launch's cabin to be absolutely sure that they didn't jerk when I fired. Nina was still talking, and I thought that it might be important. So I waited until she had stopped talking, and then I took careful aim and shot her just as you jumped."

She stopped talking for a moment, and then started again:

"I just collapsed on the launch after I had fired that one shot. I didn't even know whether I had hit her until Cleyton came and told me that she was dead. Cleyton dragged you aboard the launch, and then he sailed her farther up the coast just in case all the shooting had been heard. We hid among the ice floes at the north end of Dog Island until the trawler tracked us down on the homer signal."

It hurt Larren to speak again. He said feebly, "There's only one thing I can't understand. How did Joe know that Nina was simply stringing me along?"

Margaret Norstadt looked at him almost pitifully. "Because Joe knew women, Larren. Especially actresses. Remember that he was an ace stunt-man — he worked in films. Before the crash that messed up his face Joe had known hundreds of women. And you can't know that amount of women without learning something about them. They talk about a woman's intuition, but I guess that Joe had got so close to so many that some of that intuition rubbed off. He simply sensed something wrong about Nina Petrovitch. And when you kissed her he was sure. He was watching her eyes when Cleyton and I had left to find Otuk and she was making up to you in the hospital ward. Joe had kissed an awful lot of women, and he had seen a lot more stage kisses on the film sets — and he knew the difference. The expression in Nina's eyes changed the moment *you* were unable to see them."

The silver-grey eyes were damp again, and this time blinking did not clear them. Margaret Norstadt stood up and turned towards the cabin door. Larren did not try to stop her but thankfully allowed the darkness to creep back over his mind.

★ ★ ★

Four weeks later Simon Larren was discharged from a north London hospital. He was not one hundred per cent fit, but he was on his feet and his doctors had assured him that only the scars would be permanent. His first move was to a public call box where he dialled Whitehall 0-1-0 and asked for extension double 0. Smith told him to come up.

The paunchy little man received Larren in the book-lined office and considerately offered him a seat. Larren sat. Smith beamed at him benevolently and said:

"It's good to see you almost fit for business again, Larren. We'll have to arrange some kind of training programme, one of the refresher courses perhaps, to bring you right back to scratch. There's a job coming to a head in Tangier that just might need your special touch." He paused and gave Larren a keen look. "But that isn't what you came to hear — is it?"

Larren smiled. "Not exactly."

"All right." Smith sat down and gazed at him across the desk. "I'll tell you what happened as a result of Cleyton's report on Barren Island. It caused a lot of hurried conferences between western defence chiefs, but the final result was a secret letter, signed by representatives of both Britain and America, that was sent to Moscow. The letter revealed that we know exactly what is going on on

Barren and on its sister island in the Bering Strait. And the letter warned that any attempt to interfere with, or create false alarms, on the DEW line-warning system, would be regarded as an act of war and treated as such. There would be no recall to the Strategic Air Command or to Britain's H-bomber fleets, regardless of whether or not the false signals were switched off.

"Of course the Russians denied any such intentions. They admitted that the electronic machines were there on the two islands, but claimed that they were only to be used to cause confusion as defence measures in the event of western aggression. No doubt if war ever comes they will be used, but we are as certain as we can possibly be that they will not now be used to start a war. To be precise we have called the Soviet bluff, and I think I can safely say that we have won an Arctic Cuba."

Larren said with feeling, "I'm relieved to hear it."

Smith stood up, and spoke one of his rare words of praise, "You did a good job,

Larren. You and Cleyton. I'm sorry that my thanks are the only gratitude you can ever know."

Larren rose to leave and said quietly, "Don't thank me — or Cleyton. We were both beautifully fooled. We owe our lives to the intuition of a dead man."

THE END